D0365278

My Last Skirt

ALSO BY LYNDA DURRANT

Echohawk

The Beaded Moccasins:
The Story of Mary Campbell

Turtle Clan Journey

Betsy Zane, the Rose of Fort Henry

The Sun, the Rain, and the Apple Seed:
A Novel of Johnny Appleseed's Life

My Last Skirt

The Story of
JENNIE HODGERS, UNION SOLDIER

BY LYNDA DURRANT

CLARION BOOKS | NEW YORK

Clarion Books
a Houghton Mifflin Company imprint
215 Park Avenue South, New York, NY 10003
Copyright © 2006 by Lynda Durrant

The text was set in 12-point Elysium Book.

www.houghtonmifflinbooks.com

Printed in the U.S.A.

Library of Congress Cataloging-in-Publication Data

Durrant, Lynda, 1956–
My last skirt : the story of Jennie Hodgers, Union soldier / by Lynda Durrant.
p. cm.
Summary: Enjoying the freedom afforded her while dressing as a boy
in order to earn higher pay after immigrating from Ireland,
Jennie Hodgers serves in the 95th Illinois Infantry as Private Albert Cashier,
a Union soldier in the American Civil War.   Includes bibliographical references.
ISBN-13: 978-0-618-57490-2
ISBN-10: 0-618-57490-5
1. Hodgers, Jennie, 1843-1915—Juvenile fiction. 2. United States. Army.
Illinois Infantry Regiment, 95th (1862-1865)—History—Juvenile fiction.
3. United States—History—Civil War, 1861-1865—Juvenile fiction.
[1. Hodgers, Jennie, 1843-1915—Fiction. 2. Sex role—Fiction.
3. Soldiers—Fiction. 4. Irish Americans—Fiction. 5. United States. Army.
Illinois Infantry Regiment, 95th (1862-1865)—History—Fiction.
6. United States—History—Civil War, 1861-1865—Fiction.]   I. Title.
PZ7.D93428My 2006 [Fic]—dc22
2005027746

QUM   10   9   8   7   6   5   4   3   2

To Gary, Mark, and Martha,
and all those changing colors

CONTENTS

1

THE WHITEHEAD BRAMBLE

———

*M*Y SKIRT IS A HAND-ME-DOWN FROM my stepmother, Bridget: mud brown, linsey-woolsey, scratchy, and so long the damp and the sandy peat never leave the skirt tail, no matter how many nights it drips and steams by the fire. . . .

On feast days and after school, my brother, Tom, and I gather seashells and cockles on the shingle of the Island Magee. The flat spit of land seems to stretch a welcoming arm from our Irish shores toward Scotland. On rare sunny days we can see across the North Channel to the purple tops of mountains.

Today there're others on the shingle as well, in the soft rain and fog. We're all looking for something to sell or to eat. Shipwrecks between Ballcarry, Ireland, and Ballantrae, Scotland, are plentiful. For centuries the Irish and the Scots have sailed from one shore to the other, looking for fortunes, or fame, or freedom. Something of one or another almost always washes up.

After our noon meal of oatmeal bread and apples, it begins to rain a bit harder. The puffins, gulls, and auks fly out to sea. That means the storm is blowing in from the Lough Neagh, from the west.

"We'll take them into Belfast and sell them tomorrow." My older brother is always full of ideas for making money. "We'll take them to Donegal Quay and sell them to our own Mr. Kelly for four a penny."

I kick my wet skirt tail out from under my boots. "Mr. Kelly sells them for four a penny, Tom. He'll buy them from us for twelve a penny."

Tom turns over an empty cockleshell. The smooth inside is the same solid dark gray as a Belfast winter sky. "We'll sell them all, just you wait. A thing of beauty, isn't it?" I hold out my skirt so Tom can pile our treasure of cockles into it. "How many do we have, Jennie? How much have we made?"

I run the cockles through the fingers of my right hand while Tom pours them in. "Forty, maybe fifty. At twelve a penny that's . . ." I look out to sea while I do the figuring in my head. For me, figuring numbers has always been easy as breathing. "That's three pennies, Tom. Maybe four."

"Four pennies! We're rich!"

It's raining hard now. My skirt is heavy with the wet and the pouched cockles. The waist cuts into my back; the sodden cloth pulls me down.

"Run!" Tom shouts. He bounds over the sand dunes, the rocks, and the boulders with the other boys, as easy as a Knockmealdown Mountains stag.

I stagger along with the other girls, my soggy skirt a dead weight against my lower half. It brushes against the wet sand, picks up seaweed.

Our brothers and sweethearts, drier than we, are waiting for us girls under the roofs along the shoreline.

"What took you so long?" Tom grumbles.

"Tom! I've lost the cockles!" I cry. As I hurried to get out of the wet, the cockles bounced and jostled right out of my skirt and onto the shingle again. The wind picks up. Blowing sand and rising surf bury them faster than we could ever hope to find them. The rain spills out in sheets.

"Girls!" Tom says. "Useless creatures. Can't even carry the cockles that will bring us fame and fortune."

"It's not the girl. It's the clothes."

"Aye." Tom sighs. "We might as well wait for the weather to clear."

"And you'll have to cross the ocean for fortune, fame, and freedom, Tom."

A mistake. As soon as the words are out of my mouth, I wish I could snatch them back.

"Across the ocean—that's where fame and fortune are to be found," Tom proclaims. Several of the other boys turn to him, their faces lit up in agreement.

"Boston!" one boy shouts.

"Nay, New York. There are more Irish there than

in all of Dublin town," a second boy declares. I recognize him from school.

"My da got work on the Baltimore docks," another boy says. "Soon as school's over next year, I'm leaving to join him."

"Fame and fortune!" Tom shouts again.

Our schoolmates go on boasting about America, how there's plenty of money to be made for a man who's not afraid of hard work.

As the weather fairs, my brother starts to run, as though he's on his way to the rich cities of America right now. I pick up my water-laden skirt to follow.

"Boston, New York, or Baltimore, Jennie." Tom's voice floats behind him on the freshening wind. "Or Savannah, where the coconuts grow. The gold's just lying there on the streets, waiting for those with the pluck to pick it up. There's salmon, beef, butter, and bread on every table. Puddings so thick you must cut them with a knife. Not a ruddy potato as far as the eye can see."

"Watch what you say about the potatoes." I'm panting. "Remember the blight."

"The blight's over now, and I'll be long gone ere it ever comes back."

"Wait for me! Please."

Tom stops, then guides me under the roof of a sweetshop, closed for the day. "If you weren't a lady, I'd lift your skirt and wring it out for you."

"Lady or no, wring it out anyway. I'll never get home before dark without crawling. This skirt weighs a ton."

I stand against the sweetshop door. Folks are hurrying home, paying no mind to a colleen and her fourteen-year-old brother. Tom wrings my skirt tail out as best he can. The cold wind against my bare legs makes me shiver. I study a toffee box in the window and try to forget how cold I am.

"If there's gold just lying there in the streets, why do people in America have to work?" I wonder aloud. "Americans shouldn't have to work at all, then."

"Females!" Tom's voice is full of scorn. "They don't understand about a man's life."

"There are no coconuts in Savannah, Tom." My voice is full of scorn too. "You're thinking of cotton."

"A treasure in cockles!" My father laughs, not unkindly. We sit at table while the rain drums against our window. The rain doesn't clear the window of greasy soot. "Never mind, lad. I have good news. I can put you to work helping me shepherd the bishop's flock this summer. He'll pay you a penny a day."

Tom pulls a face, then quickly looks to the peat fire.

"I saw that face, m' boy," my father cries out. "You'll not turn up your nose at a penny a day, not from the bishop of Belfast."

"Aye." Tom's shoulders sag.

"I like sheep, Da," I say eagerly. "I like the bishop, too. I'll watch his sheep. I'd like a penny a day."

"He'll not pay you that much, Jennie." Da scowls

at Tom. "Not when there are grown men about, looking for work to feed their families."

"But I'll be feeding our family, Da."

"Jennie, you'll not be wearing your Sunday skirt out roving the bramble." Our stepmother, Bridget, sits by the fire, stirring a pot of potatoes, leeks, and mussels. "You'll not wear your second best, either."

"That settles it, then. Skirts aren't for shepherds. Tom—" my father raises his voice—"a penny a day, that's six pennies a week. The sheep are in the fold on Sundays. When school starts again, you'll watch them after. I think I could get you three pennies a week for after school."

Tom juts his chin out at the peat fire. There's more money to be made selling cockles. I know he'd rather spend his afternoons on the shingle of the Island Magee, trading stories about America with his mates while someone else counts his cockles and does his figuring for him.

I speak up again. "Nothing's settled. Tom's got a pair of old trousers that no longer fit him. I'll wear them for roving the Whitehead Bramble."

Tom, my father, and Bridget sit there, stunned.

"I'll not lie to the bishop!" my father proclaims at last. "I'll not be passing off a daughter as a son."

"No one's lying to anyone, nor will they!" I shout back. "Bishop Bannock knows me as well as he knows Tom. My brother is a businessman." I wink at Tom and he grins at me. "I like sheep, Da. It's only till the summer."

"Tom's old trousers need mending; then they're

a gift to my nephew," Bridget says. "My brother in County Kerry needs all the help we can give."

"I'll send him three pennies a week," I reply. "I like sheep, Da. I'm old enough. I'm strong enough."

My father sighs. "He'll not pay you a penny a day, m' girl."

The next morning, instead of my damp skirt, I pull Tom's old trousers over my legs. He shows me how to roll up the cuffs so they won't get wet.

I practice moving about a bit in front of the fire. It's disconcerting. When I stop, I just . . . stop. I don't have a heavy skirt trailing after, always playing catch-up. Tom's old pants are bone dry and much lighter than a linsey-woolsey skirt, damp all the time.

Bridget rolls up my hair and stuffs it into an old brimmed hat of Tom's. "It's no use ruining your complexion out on the bramble," she cautions me. "A woman's face is her fortune. And you'll thank me later for protecting your hair from the briars."

"Thank you." I gasp at my reflection in the mirror. Surely my fortune is in sheep and cockles, for under Tom's hat, I look too much like my brother for my own good. With no hair around my face to soften it, I have the same broad cheekbones and jutting chin as Tom.

Da and I sit down to a big breakfast of eggs, bacon, and oatmeal bread. I'm not used to eating so much food in the morning.

"Eat up," Da says. "A shepherd needs his

strength. I'll warn you again—the bishop won't pay you a penny a day."

Da and I walk to the bishop's farm. After yesterday's hard rain, today is a soft day of rainy fog. As the wind blows, the mist chills my face, but my legs stay warm in Tom's old trousers. I hop over stones and cairns with no thought to lifting a long skirt before I tread on the hem. I'm as free as those puffins we saw off the Island Magee, flying out to sea to avoid the storm.

The bishop's farm is closer to Carrickfergus than Ballycarry. It's a far walk. I see the thatched roof, curl of peat smoke, and stone barn long before I see the house. In the fold are his fifty-six prize merinos, milling about in a bleating sheep panic.

The bishop's sheepdogs sidle and lunge, dashing around the fences, forcing the flock into ever-smaller circles.

"Why are they herding the sheep now?" I ask. "They're still in the fold."

"Jip and Col like to show off," my father replies. "Don't you, boys?"

Old Bishop Bannock greets us at the door. "Jip! Col! That'll do. Don't worry my sheep so early in the morning." His sheepdogs trot over to the kitchen doorstep and sit, their eyes bright with self-satisfaction. The bishop gives each a pat on the head. "Patrick Hodgers! Good day to you."

"Bishop Bannock, this is—"

"I know who this is. Young Tom Hodgers." The bishop grasps my right hand and gives it a hard shake. "Come to help your da take care of the sheep, have you, m' boy? It's a man's work, and it gets you out of the factories."

I just stand there, stunned, as he pumps my arm up and down. The bishop is not wearing his glasses. Is that why he thinks I'm my brother? Before Da has a chance to set him straight, I say, "Thank you, Bishop. Thank you for the chance."

"You watch your father, young man." The bishop beams at Da. "He knows more about sheep than any man I know."

Da tries to get a word in. "Bishop, this is—"

The bishop half closes the door. "I must prepare for matins. Take them up to the cliffs of the Whitehead Bramble today, Patrick Hodgers. The meadow up there hasn't been worked over since March."

The bishop gives us a cheerful wave. The door shuts.

Da smiles uneasily at me. "We'd best get to work, then."

"Aye." I grin back at him. "For a penny a day."

Da walks me around to the barn, takes his oaken staff from the hook, and finds another staff for me. "This will help you walk the hills and dales of the bramble. It's also to protect the sheep. It's the wild dogs we shepherds have to contend with. Wild dogs and foxes have a taste for mutton."

Each staff ends in a curve like a fishhook. The hook and stout staff are as smooth as silk. "How many generations of hands have held this staff, do you suppose?"

"It's hard to say, lass. The oaks of Ireland are long gone." Da closes the barn door as the horses whinny at us. "Oliver Cromwell's soldiers cut them down two hundred years ago, so the Irish heroes couldn't take cover behind them to shoot at his men."

It's beautiful up here, roving the bramble. The sheep are white with black faces and legs. The sheepdogs are black and white as well. The fields are ever-changing shades of green, and the boulders, fog, and fence stones are gray. It's the same colors—gray, green, with flecks of white and black—wherever I look.

Da sits down on a large boulder. I sit beside him. It too is as smooth as silk. How many shepherds have sat on this boulder? Surely more than a hundred generations.

"Smell that air, Jennie. That's pure Irish air. No Belfast factory soot up here. Breathe it in. There's no finer anywhere."

"It smells sweet, Da, with a hint of peat to it. It's so quiet."

"Aye."

We sit there awhile, in perfect contentment. I hold on to my two-hundred-year-old staff as though it were a holy relic.

As they graze, the sheep spread out like a fisherman's net. The sheepdogs run in circles to draw them together again.

My father has been watching the bishop's sheep for years. He started when Old Ben was still running the fields, showing Jip the lay of the land. Now it's Jip's turn to teach Col. Every farm has three sheepdogs: the oldest, retired to the fireside; the middle one to teach the youngest.

"When the day's over, will we go to the bishop's fireside and give Old Ben a pat on the head?" I ask.

"Aye. He's always glad to see me. Old Ben and I go back ten years."

"I've always liked your stories about Old Ben, Da." After a moment I say, "What do you think about Tom's plans? To live in America?"

My father smiles. "A young man's plans, sure enough."

I look at him in surprise. "You wouldn't go with him, then?"

He spreads his arms wide. "Is there anything like this view in America?"

"I don't know. Is there really money in the streets? Gold?"

"Is that what Tom's been telling you?" Da stretches out his legs. "I'll ask you, lass: if there really were gold in the streets, every mother's son would already be there, wouldn't he?"

"Aye. And you don't mind, fooling the bishop this way?"

"As long as you do a man's day's work, we'll tell him tomorrow." He jumps down from the boulder. "That's Jip and Col, barking. A sheep must have gone over the hill and onto the ledge. This is the other part of shepherding, Jennie. Watch me."

Col has run back to us. He circles around, then

pretends to lunge at our heels. His lunging cuts us off from the boulder, forcing us toward the cliff. "He's trying to herd us, isn't he?"

Da grins. "Aye. Away to me, Col! Show me the lost one."

Col veers right, then tears off in a straight line toward the cliff, so fast I shout in alarm.

"He'll stop, even with all this mud. Good Col."

Jip and a distraught ewe are waiting for us. As we approach the cliff, I hear a faint cry. Da lies flat, then sits up again. "It's a spring lamb bleating for its mother."

Tom told me once that shepherds hold on to their mates' legs as they lower themselves down the cliff. "Will I be holding your legs, Da?"

"You're not strong enough for that, lass." Da dips the hooked end of his staff down the cliff. "I'll try to scoop the lamb up."

Da lies flat again and leans farther and farther over the cliff. I've never seen the soles of his shoes before. They're full of holes. The pad of each toe is open to the air and the same gray color as stone.

"Lamb! Come to me!"

The bleating sounds a bit louder, as though the lamb is asking for more help than Da can give. His hat blows off and spins toward the sea.

"Come to me, lamb. Your mother's up here waiting."

I sit down and grasp his ankles. "Let go, Jennie!" he calls out impatiently.

"I *am* strong enough, Da." I tighten my grip.

"I said let go!" Da kicks hard, tips forward, then slides on the mud. His ankles are in the air before I think to grasp them again. I see him flying, his right hand holding his staff, his left hand holding one of the lamb's legs as he spins toward the sea.

The ewe bleats. Jip and Col look at me expectantly, as though I have a plan for rescuing the two of them from the depths of the North Channel, and all they have to do is wait for it.

In the southwest of Ireland fishermen wear their family's patterns knitted into their sweaters. Should their bodies wash up on the shingle, families can tell who's who, even after the pebbles, seals, and surf are done with them. But everyone recognizes Patrick Hodgers.

We wake him in his own house. The burial society comes around, seals his coffin, and takes it to the churchyard.

The next day Bridget is packing her skirts, blouses, shawls, and hats into the carpetbags she brought to her marriage.

"Where you going?" Tom asks.

"My brother needs me in County Kerry—the blight's still bad there. His wife has surely died by now." Her back is turned away from us.

"We can't go to Kerry," Tom says. "We have jobs."

"We have school," I say.

Bridget doesn't even stop wrapping stockings around her hand. "You've always suited yourself,

Tom Hodgers. You can keep the skirt, Jennie. You've always been kind to me."

Tom stomps into the kitchen, grabs the cigar box, and stomps back. "How much will you be needing for your train?"

She spins around and eyes the cigar box. "Ten pounds."

"You'll need two pounds three pence to get to Cork. After that you can walk." My brother thrusts the cigar box into my hands.

They stare at me while I count the coins. All those cockles we sold to Mr. Kelly! All those months and years of Da watching sheep in all weathers! I give the coins to Tom, who throws the Hodgers' hard-earned money on the bed. Ten pounds would get to her America and back. Two pounds three is enough for a train to Cork, then a stagecoach to Dingle, County Kerry.

"That's five pounds even," I say. "There's enough for some proper food for our stepcousins besides. Thank you for the skirt."

Bridget scoops up the coins, takes her sweet time counting them out herself, and slips them into the carpetbag.

She stands in front of us. "Good luck, then."

Tom raises his chin. "Good riddance, then."

2

QUEENS

---

*F*OR THE NEXT SIX MONTHS TOM sells cockles and I wear trousers to shepherd the bishop's flock. I find some shearing scissors in the bishop's barn and cut my hair as best I can. It's Tom who asks Bishop Bannock if we can live in his barn, and clean stalls in lieu of rent. Once he gets over the shock of learning that I am Jennie, he says yes.

At the New Year, Tom and I stop going to school; we work like men and we hoard our money like pirates. But still we don't have enough to pay our way to New York this spring.

The bishop sees our long faces and gives us the rest of the money, along with plenty of advice. "The ship will let you off in what's called Castle Clinton, in southern Manhattan. You'll see a steady stream of hopefuls going to Five Points. You're not to stay there, Tom and Jennie, for it is the foulest place on God's green earth. Half of Northern Ireland is in New York now, and I hear plenty. It would break your parents' hearts to see you there."

He opens his desk drawer and cradles some coins in his hand. "Here's a bit more. That's two dollars' worth of American money to get you started. Take the ferry to the city of Brooklyn, then take the Long Island Railroad to the county of Queens. Ask for work at Albert O'Banion's Finest Groceries. I'll give you the address."

I study the American coins: red Indians on the coppers; lasses draped in flowing robes like angels, but carrying the Banner of Stars before them, on the silvers. The lasses on the silvers have wings sprouting from their temples or crowns of laurel leaves in their flowing hair. Not a king or queen in the lot. The coppers are full pennies and half pennies, just as in Ireland.

The biggest coin says *Five Cents;* the smallest, *Ten Cents.*

"Why is the bigger one worth half of the smaller?"

The bishop shrugs. "It's America, Jennie."

"How do you know Albert O'Banion?" Tom asks.

"He was a parishioner of mine when I was the Ballynure parish priest. He's done well in New York. I'll write you a letter of introduction."

"Tom! Look at this!" I show my brother the wording on the five-cent piece: *The United States of America.* "It's like we're already there."

"Jennie," the bishop says sternly, "dressing as a boy—I hope you give up such foolishness once you're in New York. Women and girls are a civilizing influence in every nation. It is my opinion that America needs all the civilizing it can get."

Tom says, "You said go to Queens. But there's no Queen of America."

"No, no, lad. The county of Queens was named after Queen Catherine of Portugal, married to England's Charles II."

Tom frowns. "Why would they be naming a patch of America after a queen from Portugal?"

The bishop shrugs. "It's America," he says again. "Don't take an Irish or British ship for your crossing. They're not called coffin ships for nothing. Take an American ship, or a Dutch or German one. They leave Belfast, then cross the Atlantic from Liverpool.

"Did you hear me, Jennie? No more dressing like a boy."

"Aye, I heard you."

The bishop stares at me and waits. Finally, he asks, "Do I have your promise?"

Tom speaks up. "Don't make her give you her promise. We'll need the money she earns in America. She'll give it up once we're settled."

"Jennie?"

"Once we're settled, Bishop Bannock." *Maybe*.

"That'll have to do. I'll give you both my blessing."

———

Eight weeks later we're in Queens. We've never seen such a place as this. If jobs are the gold we seek, then the streets are paved with them: chimney sweeps, bone boilers, charcoal makers, coachmen, iron workers, tanners, blacksmiths, shop clerks, soap makers, lamplighters, coal-oil distillers, garbagemen, policemen, firemen, icemen, footmen, trolley conductors, bakers, pharmacists, teachers, nurses, doctors, lawyers, confectioners, butchers, bakers, cooks, laundresses, seamstresses, clothes steamers, millinery workers, scullery maids, nannies, butlers, chefs, waiters, waitresses, bartenders, and barmaids.

New York is bursting at the seams. Everyone's in a hurry: It's rush to the job, rush home for the dinner, rush out for the amusements, and rush home again. Perhaps they've found a way to rush sleep as well.

Everywhere there are vast herds of goats, of all things, thousands of them. The Dutch farmers used to keep them, two hundred years ago. The goats have gone wild long since.

Mr. O'Banion sets us to work—Tom and me as his younger brother, Georgie—as soon as we show him Bishop Bannock's letter. We're real Yankee Doodles now, for Tom and I have three jobs between us: We're clerks and broom pushers. We take turns sleeping in the back of the store to spend our nights guarding the Finest Groceries as well.

It's just after Christmas, a cold January morning. Tom and I have been in America for seven months now. Mr. O'Banion is stirring the milk to break the ice and pouring it out into bottles for the Monday-morning rush. I'm stoking the Franklin stove in the middle of the store.

I can hear Mrs. Coombs's boys long before I can see them. Then Mrs. Coombs's twin three-year-olds and her five-year-old burst through the shop door and run off in three different directions. Tom and I cringe as grubby hands reach into the pickle barrel. The twins commence to throw bread rolls at each other, as though they're engaged in a snowball fight.

"Tom, Georgie," Mr. O'Banion calls. "Perhaps you could take the boys outside for a bit of fresh air?"

It's just then that old Mrs. Zimmerhosten comes into the grocery, as ornery a customer as a crab in a stew pot. She grabs a loaf of bread from the bin and pushes me toward the cash drawer.

"*Schnell! Schnell!*" she snarls at me. She pokes me in the stomach with her coins. "I buy de *Brot* now."

I whisper, "I've never worked the cash drawer, Mrs. If you could just wait for Mr. O'Banion—"

"*Dummkopf* Irish! *Schnell! Schnell!* I buy de *Brot* NOW!"

I don't know what *Dummkopf* means. It can't be flattery, not with the way her eyes are popping out at me. But I've watched Mr. O'Banion work the cash drawer a hundred times.

I wind the crank, and the drawer flies open. The bell rings. Mrs. Zimmerhosten slaps two nickels on the counter.

"Dree cents back I get, young man."

"I've got good news, Mrs. Zimmerhosten. That's yesterday's bread you're holding. It's only four cents."

I give her back one nickel and one penny and close the cash drawer with a bang.

She glares suspiciously at me. "Yesterday's *Brot?*"

I point to the sign above the bread bin. "That says, 'Yesterday's bread.' We don't have today's in yet."

She looks at the sign with no light of recognition in her eyes.

She can't read English!

"Yesterday's bread. Yesterday's *Brot*." I hold up four fingers. "Four cents."

Mr. O'Banion comes running over. "Who said you could open the cash drawer, Georgie?" he asks angrily.

"I'm sorry, Mr. O'Banion, but she kept yelling *'Schnell! Schnell!'* I've given her the right change."

Mrs. Zimmerhosten gives Mr. O'Banion a huge smile. I've never seen her happy before. "'Yesterday's bread. Four cents only,' Georgie says."

"Right you are, Mrs. Zimmerhosten."

"Oh, no!" I gasp. "That's Saturday's bread, sir. It's *two* days old."

"Mrs." With a flourish, Mr. O'Banion gives her another loaf. "A service to you. This is, um . . . *Samstag's Brot. Samstag?*"

"*Danke!*" She holds up that saved nickel. "Tomorrow I buy two *Brot!*" She pats my hand. "Dis good boy." She leaves the grocery just as the Coombs twins are fighting over who gets to open the door.

"*Ach!* In de store should *Kinder verboten* be!" Mrs. Zimmerhosten shoots Mrs. Coombs a look that could freeze the Devil in his tracks. She pushes the door open, sending one of the twins onto the sidewalk with a howl.

"You've got a new job, Georgie," Mr. O'Banion shouts over the ruckus. "You're in charge of charming Mrs. Zimmerhosten. And you'll stand the cash drawer when I'm busy."

"Thank you, Mr. O'Banion."

"You have a way with figures. It's a gift, Georgie."

Tom watches me from behind the butter barrel. Mr. O'Banion keeps fresh butter afloat in a barrel of ice water. Tom's look is as frozen as the butter.

Just before Easter Mr. O'Banion gives me a present. "Here's two tickets to the Olympic Theatre in Manhattan, 585 Broadway. You've worked so hard, Georgie. But now you'll work harder—you'll laugh so hard, your sides will split. Wait until you hear Izzie and Iggie! And I used to think we Irish were funny. No more."

"We're funny," Tom retorts.

"Aye, Tom, just not *as* funny. You'll see." My employer smiles at me. "I want to give you a present for being such a good cashier, Georgie. You'll get a raise, too."

"Thank you, sir!" I beam at Tom, and he scowls back.

That Wednesday evening I treat Tom and myself

to the Long Island Railroad southwest to Brooklyn, then the ferry into Manhattan.

The Olympic is a grand affair. There are red carpets on the floors and rose-red velvet seats trimmed in gold in the lobby. The staircases are marble, with little rugs stuck onto each tier so the patrons can't slip. Marble statuary crowds the corners.

Squawk! Such a pretty bird! Pretty bird!

"Jennie, look at this!" Tom calls out. His eyes are huge. There in the middle of the lobby is a birdcage with two parrots in it, their feathers as green as shamrocks. They regard us with keen intelligence in their shining black eyes.

I stare in wonder at the parrots, and then my gaze wanders up to the ceiling: Against a blue-black background, painted gold stars in the patterns of constellations shine overhead.

"Have you ever seen anything so grand?" Tom whispers. "It's like a sultan's palace in here."

"It is grand. Tom, don't call me Jennie," I whisper. "I'm Georgie."

"I'll call you what I like."

A gong sounds and the gaslights dim. We find seats in the middle of the theater.

The show is something called a review. There are jugglers, and acrobats who can twist and turn like pretzels. Dogs with frilly collars jump onto huge balls and roll them around the stage. A magician pulls rabbits out of his hat and saws his pretty wife in half. Two black men come onstage and commence to dance—so fast is their fancy footwork, they sound like driving rain on a tin roof.

Between the acts we watch line dancers with crowns of pink feathers in their hair.

Two women go on and sing a song about the American South: "Look away, look away, look away, Dixieland." Their voices are as sweet and pure as bells, but the men in the balcony boo them and their song. "The Union! The Union!" the men shout. A tomato lands with a *splat* on the stage. The women leave the boards in tears.

"Tom, look away from what, I wonder? Why didn't the balcony boys enjoy their singing?"

But Tom has something else on his mind. "Where're the funny bits?" he complains. "Why aren't my sides splitting? Mr. O'Banion was wrong, wasn't he?"

Two men dressed in fancy evening clothes come onstage. They introduce themselves as Izzie and Iggie Washingtonstein. They tell rare stories and trade insults. They make fun of all the kinds of people there are in New York, and we all laugh together, even when the jokes are at our own expense. Tom and I laugh so hard, we can barely hear the next joke. Every time we're supposed to laugh, someone backstage pounds a drum. *Boom!*

Izzie says, "An Irishman once told me, 'My wife says I drink too much. "Paddy," she says, "when you've had enough whiskey, you should ask for sarsaparilla." "Rosie," I told her, "when I've had enough whiskey, I can't *say* sarsaparilla."'"

Boom!

Iggie says, "You should see my neighbor's daughter, Izzie. Isabella Christosanti's got a face so ugly, it could stop a clock."

Izzie says, "No, she's a lucky girl, Iggie. Think of all the time she'll have now to find a husband."

Boom!

Izzie says, "Two bank robbers named Hans and Fritz try to hide their loot by dumping it in the middle of the East River. Hans throws the bag of silver dollars over the side of their rowboat. It sinks like a stone."

"'Hans, you *Dummkopf!*' Fritz yells. 'You've lost our money.' Hans tosses one of the oars overboard. 'Not to worry, Fritz,' says Hans, as he points to the oar. 'We'll come back to this very spot tomorrow and get it back.'"

Boom!

Iggie says, "A Jewish immigrant goes into a kosher restaurant on Delancey Street. The waiter who poured his water was Chinese! More than that . . . the waiter proceeded to rattle off the menu in fluent Yiddish!

"When the diner was paying his bill, he said to the cashier, 'I certainly enjoyed my dinner—and even more, the fact that your Chinese waiter speaks such excellent Yiddish.'

"Whispered the cashier, 'Shh! He thinks we're teaching him English!'"

Boom!

All around us, men and their sweethearts are roaring with laughter, weeping with laughter. Tom hangs on to my arm and laughs so hard that I can tell he's forgotten whatever it is he's so angry with me about.

As our second summer in America passes, I stand behind the cash drawer as the head cashier. I know every customer by name. I know to whom to give credit and who has to pay in cash each time.

Mr. O'Banion now pays me half again as much as Tom. Dollars, fifty-cent pieces, quarters, dimes, nickels, pennies, and half pennies fill up the cigar box, so we get another box for the extra. We buy all our food for a discount at our employer's Finest Groceries. We don't have to pay any rent because we guard the store at night. Not even Da ever had so much money at one time in his whole life.

Every Friday we go to the First Bank of New York and exchange our coins for bills.

One Saturday Mr. O'Banion gives us the afternoon off to buy some clothes. "It won't do to have my clerks in rags. Go to my tailor, Mr. Russo, on the Shore Road. He's the best tailor in Queens. Nobody makes men's haberdashery like those Italians."

Mr. O'Banion slaps a ten-dollar bill on the counter, then rushes to the front of the store. The Coombs boys and their mother have arrived.

I scoop up the money. "Ten dollars! We could buy clothes as fine as Izzie and Iggie's. Won't we be a sight now?"

Tom casts me a dark look. "We're settled, aren't

we, Jennie? Are you forgetting the promise you made to Bishop Bannock?"

"I made no such promise, and don't call me Jennie. I'm Georgie. Why aren't you happy, Tom? We're in America, just as you wanted. And it's grand. Isn't it grand, Tom?"

"I'll call you what I like."

3

JUST A JOKE

Y BODY BEGINS TO CHANGE AS THE summer ripens into autumn. My waist gets smaller and my hips grow wider. My breasts start growing.

My beautiful tweed jacket (bought with my own money that I earned as Mr. O'Banion's head cashier) no longer lies flat against my chest. I have to hunch my shoulders forward to create a hollow in front.

I picked out the tweed myself. The subtle shades of greens and grays in the weave reminded me of the Whitehead Bramble back home. The wool is soft, without a touch of prickle in it.

Mr. Russo nodded his approval as he took up the fabric between his thumb and fingers. "You have a fine hand and a keen eye for cloth, Georgie Hodgers," he said to me. "I'd hire you as a fabric buyer tomorrow."

The jacket will have to go to the St. Brendan's jumble sale soon. So will the wonderfully soft shirts of Sea Pine Island cotton that Mr. Russo made just for me. Unless I do something drastic.

But what can I do? I can't stop time itself.

I don't have to worry about below the waist. Tom buys our underdrawers from Mr. O'Sullivan's Finest Dry Goods and General Store. I don't have to try them on first. Mr. Russo made my trousers with room to grow.

I don't know what I'm going to do about my upper half.

If Mr. O'Banion finds me out, surely he'll dismiss me on the spot. I wonder if he'd call a policeman as well? I'm certainly not who I claim to be.

And yet, I am myself. Aren't I? I'm Georgie Hodgers, with nothing to apologize for. I wear beautiful clothes and I'm proud to be working three jobs in America. Once we land on this golden shore, we decide who we want to be. That's why we're in America in the first place. We are who we say we are.

Aren't we?

Tom and I have Sunday dinner at the O'Banions' every week, and on feast days as well. They're as close to family as we have now. The O'Banions have six children, better behaved than the Coombs boys to be sure, but their house is still a bit on the rough-and-tumble side.

This Sunday I spy a catalogue in Mrs. O'Banion's knitting basket. *Mrs. Windermere's "My Constant Com-*

panion" *Foundations and Intimate Apparel,* says the cover. Mrs. O'Banion is in the kitchen with her two daughters, mashing the potatoes and carving the beef. The O'Banion boys are wrestling with my brother on the parlor floor. Mr. O'Banion is reading the Sunday newspaper, oblivious to the commotion.

I slip out the back door with the *Constant Companion* catalogue under my shirt. I hide it in the box hedge to retrieve and look at later.

That evening I study all the daguerreotypes. I read all the captions and sound out all the words. I wonder if God in Heaven will strike me down, looking at this picture book on His day of all days, and a stolen book as well.

All the modeling ladies have their eyes averted from the camera—no surprise there, for they are all wearing corsets, and drawstring bustles, and all-in-ones, and corselets, with nothing but cotton or silk chemises underneath. Black stockings reach just above the knee. Their thighs look as smooth as those marble statues at the Olympic Theatre.

These constant companions, as Mrs. Windermere calls them, are held together with silk ropes, metal buckles, garters, and whalebones with holes drilled into the sides for the laces. The crinolines are made with stout iron tines that look like spokes within a wagon wheel.

Is this what the ladies wear under all those layers of skirts, blouses, dresses, and shawls? I had no idea, no idea at all. For it's with these bustles and corsets that the ladies decide who they're going to be.

But none of these constant companions will do, for they all hoist up and boost out what I want to damp down.

Winding cloth, I think. The winding cloth of the dead would serve my purpose. Where could I find winding cloth? I know no one in the funeral business well enough to ask.

It is on the back pages, at last, that I find *my* constant companion. A smallish corselet—"for the petite woman of discriminating refinement"—with ties in the front that I can fasten myself.

I could tie such a contraption around my chest, not around my hips. My tweed jacket and shirts will lie flat again!

But how on earth do I buy such a thing? I can't walk into Mrs. Windermere's shop—not as Georgie Hodgers, I can't. A man in a ladies' foundation shop! It would be as though the very earth stood still.

I won't go as Jennie. I'll not waste good money on a dress and crinoline I'd wear only once. Besides, how could I go to Mrs. O'Banion's dressmaker's in Mr. Russo's shirts, jacket, and trousers? Again, the very earth would stand still.

I don't know where Mrs. Windermere's shop is, anyway. I've taken the horse trolley to Brooklyn, I've taken ferries to Manhattan and as far away as Staten Island, but unless she sells her dainties around New York City, I'm at a loss.

On the very last page is a sale coupon: Name, address, cash or money order.

Just below is:

Mrs. Windermere says, "I guarantee safe, discreet, and *confidential* posts for our valued clientele who do not reside in Philadelphia. You may place your order with us in fullest confidence. Simply add another dollar for the cost of postage and handling and include it with your order."

Mail order! I've heard of such things. You can buy anything you want by post in America. It's because of all those pioneers and settlers out in the wilderness, who don't live anywhere near towns and stores. What a country!

I can't write *Georgie Hodgers* on the order blank. I write *G. Hodgers, c/o O'Banion's Finest Groceries,* and the address.

Every dawn I sweep the sidewalk in front of the Finest Groceries and watch for our postman, Mr. Merriman.

"Parcel for you, Georgie," Mr. Merriman says a few weeks later. It is wrapped in plain brown paper, no bigger than a veal chop. I slip the package into my jacket pocket.

I wait until Tom is busy slicing cheese and duck into the back of the grocery. In a flick of a lamb's tail, I've got my constant companion laced around my chest. It's perfect—not a bulge in sight and nothing jiggling.

Even with my shoulders flung back, my shirt lies flat again. I'll have to wait until this evening to try on my tweed jacket.

"Thank you," I whisper. "Thank you, Mrs. Windermere. I'll say a special prayer for you this Sunday."

Only later in the day do I realize that the corselet has whalebones the size of knife blades stitched into the layers of fabric. I have to stand as straight as a soldier all that day. As the weeks pass, I wriggle the bones out bit by bit.

In November we celebrate the feast of All Saints' Day, and the next day, All Souls' Day. We sit in church for hours. I think about Ma and Da, long gone and at rest across the ocean. Tom is sitting next to me. He wipes tears away angrily with the back of his hand.

The last time Da saw me, I was dressed as a boy. What would Ma think, I wonder, to see me with my hair shorn, and dressed as though I were Tom's little brother? Would she even know me? That I'm her daughter, her own little Jennie Margaret Hodgers?

She'd understand—of course she would. Tom and I are all alone in the world, and we need all the help we can get. Ma knows that I'm still me; surely my own true self shines through yet.

I could be Jennie again—in truth, jobs for women are plentiful around New York. But the pay is next to nothing. Businessmen are always studying the young men for pluck and gumption; our city needs those who aren't afraid of hard work. I'm sure there are plenty of young women who aren't afraid of hard work, either. I've never seen the businessmen study young women—well, not in the same manner they study Tom and me, at any rate.

Despite the solemnity of this morning's Mass, dinner with the O'Banions in the late afternoon is the usual rowdy affair.

We've had smoked salmon and watercress on buttered tea bread as a starter. A fine corned beef, and plenty of baked potatoes to pass around. There are fresh Brussels sprouts, rushed by train from one of the Carolinas—North? South? East? West? Mr. O'Banion told us which one, but I forget.

A tipsy trifle waits on the sideboard.

My employer stands up and raps his spoon gently on the whiskey glass at his side. His family falls silent. He lifts his glass, full of Andrew Watts's best. "Where would this family be without the Hodgerses?" he asks. "Georgie is a wonder, the best cashier and clerk I've ever had. He's first up and sweeping the sidewalk in front of the store before I even open for business. There's never so much as a penny missing when he's standing the cash drawer."

Mr. O'Banion looks around the table cheerfully. He gives me a nod. He turns to Tom, and his face falls when he sees Tom's glaring back at him.

"Then there's Tom Hodgers," Mr. O'Banion stammers. As his hand lowers, some of his whiskey sloshes onto the lace tablecloth. I look at my brother with a pounding heart. His face is becoming darker by the moment.

Tom, if you worked harder, Mr. O'Banion would be toasting you, too.

"Tom does a fine job slicing cheese . . . and . . . and he's learning to carve blocks of butter by the pound. He'll do a fine job someday. I mean . . . he's a fine worker now." Mr. O'Banion raises his whiskey again. "To the Hodgers brothers."

Tom's face is as red as a Christmas stocking. He turns to me; his blue eyes are like bright chunks of ice.

"'Tis a shame my sister Jennie's got a face so ugly, it could stop a clock." His voice is shaking.

"Tom! No!"

"But she shouldn't worry—think of all the time she'll have now to find a husband."

I stare at Tom, too stunned to speak. Tom glares back and raises his chin.

"You're jealous of me," I say in a low voice. "You're jealous of my success in America. Mr. O'Banion gave me the raise because I work harder than you."

"*I'm* the Yankee Doodle! Coming here was *my* idea, not yours." As Tom surges to his feet, his chair falls on the rug with a dull thud.

I jump to my feet, too. "You've never swept the sidewalk at dawn. You've never bothered to learn any of the customers' names. You still think you're going to find gold in the streets, like some green-horn right off the boat—"

"I'm the Yankee Doodle, *not you!*"

"There's no gold, Tom!" I shout. "There're three jobs and more money than Da ever had in his life."

Mr. O'Banion clears his throat.

Tom's face is now beet red with rage. "That's another thing. Da's death was your fault," he says in a voice as bitter as salt. "You shouldn't have been up there, roving the Whitehead Bramble. Girls can't be shepherds."

"It wasn't a job you'd take on!"

"What is all this?" Mr. O'Banion asks.

"I grabbed his ankles. He wouldn't let me help him. That's when he slid into the North Channel! He refused my help! It *wasn't* my fault."

Tom's hands are in fists. "You might as well have pushed him off the bramble yourself, Jennie Margaret Hodgers."

"How can you say that to me?" I whisper.

"Tom? What are you saying?" Mr. O'Banion asks.

"Didn't you know about my sister? Thinks she's a man, she does. Go on, Jennie, show them!" Tom steals a glance at Mrs. O'Banion. Mrs. O'Banion just sits there, her forked potato halfway to her mouth. "Show them that . . . pink thing you wear on top. Hand-washes it late at night when she thinks I won't notice."

"Jennie?" Mr. O'Banion says. He looks at me as though seeing me for the first time. "You're *Jennie* Hodgers?"

The O'Banion brothers stare at me open-mouthed, the O'Banion sisters more open-mouthed still.

A horse-drawn trolley passes out front: *clipclop, clipclop, clipclop.* The clock on the mantelpiece ticks.

My tears turn the O'Banions into blurs.

"Aw, look at her now, crying like the girl she is," Tom jeers. "Can't you take a joke, Jennie? It's just a joke."

"Albert," Mrs. O'Banion exclaims, "did you know about this?"

"No," my employer whispers. "I never suspected a thing."

It's hard to breathe. "I'm Georgie, Georgie Hodgers. I'm . . . I'm . . ."

I flee the table, knocking into furniture because I'm crying so hard. I run down the stairs, across the yard, and to the back door of the Finest Groceries.

Money. I need money. I cram both cigar boxes into my satchel. *Too bad, Tom—you'll just have to work harder to earn your share back.* My shirts, my belts, my felt fedora, my suspenders, socks, underdrawers, everything I can I shove into the bag.

My tweed jacket has the softest leather under the lapels. Calfskin it is. It's just the thing to turn up to my chin for a cold evening's run to the train station.

"Here's one hundred and seventy dollars." I empty a cigar box onto the counter. "How far can I go with that?"

The ticket master looks up at me through eyebrows as bushy as a squirrel's tail. "You could go to the California gold fields, lad, in your own private coach and back again. Take the Long Island Railroad to the Brooklyn ferry, take the ferry to New Jersey, then ride trains down to New Orleans, then a ship around South America—"

36

"No, no. Where else have you got?"

The ticket master regards me for a moment. "You're Irish?"

"Aye. So are you."

"Is this your money? Look me in the eye with your answer, lad."

"Oh, aye, this is my money, all right. I have three jobs—clerk, cashier, and night watchman. I—I *had* three jobs."

"First, put so much money away," he whispers. "There're thieves about this night."

"Yes, sir." I sweep the bills back into the cigar box.

"My family came over from County Clare. Do you know the Clearys, then?"

"No, sir." I glance at the main door. I've got all our money. Tom could be coming through that door at any moment with murder in his eyes.

"Aye, the Clearys left County Clare, but long before the blight took the starving ones to Heaven. I've been in America for thirty years gone now. My brother and I helped build the canal out of Albany, then the railroad out to Toledo." He smiles at me. "That's Toledo, Ohio, lad, not Toledo, Spain. 'Twas hard work for a day's pay, let me tell you."

I glance at the main door again. *The Irish!* I think bitterly. *They will tell their stories!*

"My brother bought a grand farm in northern Illinois, in Boone County. He was working on the Chicago & North Western Railway. That's where the rails stopped when the money ran out one summer.

He decided to stay. A pretty farm it is, too, near the town of Belvidere—just two hours by train from Chicago.

"My brother grows oats, which he sells to the Schumacher—"

Mr. Cleary will help me. He will give me a chance. All I need is the patience to wait for it.

"—Oatmeal Company out of Akron, Ohio. Ferdinand Schumacher buys his entire crop. My brother has to go to the store to buy his own oatmeal! Have you ever heard of such a thing? Plus corn, melons, squash, pumpkins, beans—"

"Mr. Cleary!" I try to keep the irritation out of my voice. "Is there a train leaving for your brother's farm soon?"

Mr. Cleary jerks his thumb toward a steaming train. "Aye. Track seven will get you to the ferry to New Jersey, then take a train from the Jersey City station, with changes in Buffalo, Detroit, and Chicago. Are you looking for work, then?"

I stand up straight and throw back my shoulders. "I'm always looking for work."

"There's a good lad. You're a bit scrawny for farm work, though. Have you been to the Midwest?"

I give him a grim laugh. "For two years now I've been in America and I've never been out of New York State. Too busy working. But I worked as a shepherd for the bishop of Belfast. Does your brother have sheep?"

"No sheep. The winters are so cold, you'll think Hell's frozen over. The summers are so hot, you'll think Hell's thawed out again to celebrate the Fourth of July. Blizzards, tornadoes, floods, droughts, heat waves—why people are flocking to Illinois is beyond me. Good soil, though. Anything and everything grows there.

"Tell you what, lad. I'll wire my brother and tell him you're coming. You look like a good worker. What's your name?"

"Thank you, Mr. Cleary. Thank you for the chance."

My mind races for a moment. Mr. Albert O'Banion's praise echoes in my mind: *Georgie is a wonder, the best cashier and clerk I've ever had.*

I can never be Georgie Hodgers again. Tom will search to the ends of the earth for his money.

"My name is Albert, Mr. Cleary. Albert Cashier."

4

THE SIXTY-DOLLAR BOUNTY

THE BELVIDERE STANDARD
AUGUST 5, 1862

ILLINOIS'S MR. LINCOLN AND THE GRAND ARMY OF THE REPUBLIC NEED THE MEN OF BOONE COUNTY!

AN IMPORTANT ANNOUNCEMENT

The Boone County Board of Supervisors has called out a subscription of $60.00, to be deposited in the First Bank of Chicago, for each man who enlists in the Grand Army of the Republic from our county.

All able-bodied men are asked to report to the Belvidere courthouse *tomorrow,* Wednesday, August 6, at seven o'clock in the morning to muster in.

Company G has already selected officers for their grand adventure, and a finer body of men we have never seen together. In fact, if Mr. Thomas Humphrey and Mr. Elliot Bush had had their pick of the county, their success could not have been better.

"Sixty dollars, Albert," my good chum, Charlie Ives, says to me. "I've never seen that much money in my life."

"I haven't seen such money since I left Queens."

It's our day off from farm work, and we are standing on the sidewalk in front of the *Standard*'s newspaper offices. The recruitment announcement has been posted to their front window amid red, white, and blue bunting and a daguerreotype of President Abraham Lincoln.

After two years in the Midwest, my lilting brogue is gone. No more up-and-down, up-and-down speech for me, like the rising and falling of the Whitehead Bramble. I've learned to talk flat—as flat as the Illinois prairies. When I came out from Queens, no one could understand a word I said. Not even my employer, Mr. Cleary, who was born in County Clare.

I listened carefully to the speech of Americans born out here. All those *er*'s in their words reminded me of a train's engine trying to get started on a cold morning: *er, er, er, er, er.*

And yet, when I'm distracted or agitated, my Irish brogue comes rushing back, like the spring floods on the Piscasaw River. I wonder if my brogue would come back if Johnny Reb were to start shooting at me.

"Queens, New Yorrrk," I repeat, my *r*'s like gravel on the back of my tongue.

"I heard you the first time," Charlie says crossly. "Let's go! A grand adventure, it says here. I've never been out of Boone County. I haven't seen the world the way you have."

"I could put my sixty dollars in the bank."

"Aw, spend it, Albert, for once in your life! We're signing up, aren't we? You're a soldier now!"

"I never said I'm signing up."

"It would be good to leave for a spell." Here Charlie drops his voice to a whisper. "Sheriff McCutcheon suspects it's us tipping over the outhouses."

I grin. "He doesn't know about tipping over the cows as they sleep, then? But Charlie, what if the Rebs start shooting at us?"

"We'll shoot back." Charlie stares at me. "You're not scared, are you?"

This question is guaranteed to get my blood up. Any boy would take tea with the Devil himself rather than admit to being scared of anything. "Of course not!" I retort. "Who'd be scared of a bunch of scrawny Rebs?"

"I'll see you at seven tomorrow morning, Albert. Sharp."

"Sharp it is. A grand adventure." My heart starts to hammer against my constant companion.

I go back to Mr. Cleary's farm to say goodbye. He's out in the fields with his draft Shires, harvesting his first crop of oats this year.

Just this April he taught me to scour the sod with his plow. After this harvest he'll scour the sod again and plant another crop of oats for a second harvest in early November.

When I tell him my intentions, he stomps his foot on his own black soil in disgust. "Don't leave the farm, Albert. Why, you're more than three hundred miles from the nearest slave. Have you ever seen one in your life?"

"No, sir."

"Slavery's a relic, left over from when the English had colonies on the eastern seaboard. Let the American-born dodge the bullets. Don't you understand? It's not an Irishman's fight. Stay here, lad. There's plenty of work. Once the recruits go, there'll be nothing but women left in Boone County. How are we farmers going to get the crops in? How am I going to get the next harvest in? How am I going to break the new ground?"

I look over Mr. Cleary's fields, the sturdy green plants with golden tassels tossing in the prairie breeze. I've never seen soil so black and rich as here.

There's not a rock in sight to crowd the roots. Plants burst out of the earth, even bigger and healthier than the year before. "You've got your wife, and your three daughters," I reply.

"Busting sod isn't women's work."

"President Lincoln is from Illinois. He needs our help."

"He's from Kentucky," my employer argues back. "His wife's family is one of the biggest slave holders in the Bluegrass. He doesn't need your help."

"I love this country, Mr. Cleary. It's given me everything."

"Aye," he replies sadly. He reaches out to shake my hand. His are rough farmer's hands, with the earth so ground into the palms that they'll ne'er be scrubbed pink again. "Pay close attention when they teach you how to shoot. Keep your head down in battle, Albert. You're smaller than most. That'll help. And come back home to us when this war is over. I've often thought of you as the son I never had."

"Why . . . why, thank you, sir."

I walk forward and give his mares, Cheese and Crackers, four strokes on the nose each. "Goodbye," I whisper into their ears, which are the size of corncobs. The horses gaze down at me with placid brown eyes. Just like everything else in America, Cheese and Crackers are oversized, massive, and bursting with health.

He thinks of me as his son.

It still jars to know I've done such a fine job

keeping my secret safe. It jars even more to know how easy it is. Men wear trousers and women don't. People are too busy with their own affairs to look any further into the matter than that.

Mr. Cleary comes toward me, stroking Crackers's flanks. "Come back to us, lad, and I'll give you my blessing to marry one of my daughters. . . . You needn't look so shocked, Albert. I'd like to keep the farm in the family."

"I—I've never thought of your daughters in that way, sir," I stammer. "I think of them as sisters."

"You may change your mind after living in a soldiers' camp for months on end. Have you money for a Belvidere boarding-house bed this night?"

"Yes, sir."

Mr. Cleary slaps me on the back. "This war will be over soon—you can rely on it. In time we'll blockade the rivers and ports, and the Rebs will run out of everything. They'll have to give up secession then. We'll welcome them back as brothers, and we'll all have to try to forgive and forget.

"When the oats are in, I'll go into town and pay your bounty in full. You're worth sixty dollars to this family, free and clear."

"Thank you." My voice chokes. "Goodbye." I step away from the team.

"Cheese, forward. Team, haw!"

Cheese first, then Crackers. Their massive bodies step forward, then turn left on a dime. It's as though Mr. Cleary is nothing but a cornhusk doll and his iron McCormick plow no more than a soup plate.

These draft Shires don't even know how strong they are.

Tears sting my eyes. I turn away before Mr. Cleary can see me.

I can never, never come back to this farm! Not if Mr. Cleary wants to marry me off to Catherine, or Rose, or Fiona. I can never see these good, kind people again. I'm leaving yet another family behind. In horror, I wonder if the Cleary girls have ever looked at me or thought of me as more than a brother.

Surely not.

And yet I'm free, freer than Catherine, or Rose, or Fiona will ever be. Or the O'Banion sisters, either, come to think of it. Girls don't even know what freedom is. I can't imagine going back to a life of wet, muddy skirts pulling me down at every step and my labor worth a fraction of a man's.

Goodbye, the Clearys. I wipe my eyes and head to the farmhouse.

My clothes are my freedom, but I've long since learned that I can't cry. Not just because boys don't cry, but because my constant companion won't give me the air I need for the sobs. Jennie would surely be sobbing by now.

Mrs. Windermere's all-in-ones, corselets, and iron-ribbed crinolines are prison bars, sure enough, but keeping a girl's spirit inside a man's clothes is prison bars of a sort as well.

The next morning Charlie Ives and I join the Illinois 95th, Company G, Infantry. If we're to believe our own Lieutenant Colonel Humphrey, it's the best company in the entire Grand Army of the Republic.

We rush out of the boarding house to be on time for our enlistment. On my very first day of army life, I learn its first rule: "Hurry up and wait." At seven o'clock there are three hundred of us standing in line in front of the courthouse as the sun breaks over Belvidere Commons. Boone County has given President Lincoln all the men he wanted. The families here will pay our bounties by subscriptions, five or ten dollars a month to a soldiers' fund in the First Bank of Chicago. We'll each get thirteen dollars a month from the federal government whether we're fighting or not; we soldiers can draw on the bounty or have it waiting for us when we return.

I decide to keep my bounty for when I'm mustered out.

Everyone has already said his goodbyes. There are no families or sweethearts among us.

We stand in line for hours. The August sun gets hotter by the minute.

I hadn't thought about standing in front of army doctors for a physical. As I get closer to the recruitment tent, I watch in horror as doctors ask men at random to take off their shirts. They tap chests and listen to heartbeats. With no females around, the inductees strip in the open air to change into Union blue.

"Hurry it along!" Captain Bush yells. "We've got a train to catch."

I've been listening to the men state their name, age, hair and eye color, and so on. If I give my particulars quickly, maybe the doctor will let me alone.

A doctor turns to me. "Your name?" he barks.

I rattle off quickly, "Albert Cashier. Age: eighteen. Height: five feet three. Hair: auburn. Eyes: blue. Marital status: single. Occupation: farmer. Nativity: New Yorrrk." I make sure he hears that *er*. I'm not sure they'd take someone from Ireland, and I've heard from Charlie that eighteen is the age President Lincoln is looking for. He's going to claim to be eighteen as well. In truth, I have no idea how old I am.

The doctor snorts. "You don't look eighteen and you don't sound like you're from New York. They all say *Noo Yawk*."

I think quickly. "I've lived in Illinois for a long time, sir. Sirrr."

The doctor snorts again. "That's a good answer, Private Cashier. Pick out a uniform. Next!" The luck of the Irish! Just like that, I'm in the Grand Army of the Republic.

The smallest uniform I can find fits easily over my shirt and constant companion. The bright blue coat hangs almost to my knees. I make sure my coat is buttoned and my thighs are covered before I pull the gunmetal gray trousers on. I have to roll up the cuffs. Even the smallest of the caps falls to my ears.

The boots are finest leather, but even the smallest pair I can find are too big. I decide to use my farmer's boots until they wear out. I'll need a second pair of boots for winter. I can wear two pairs of socks with the army boots.

We each get a haversack with full kit: a plate, a canteen already full of water, and tableware all made of tin; a bedroll; two towels; two washcloths; regulation soap; two pairs of underdrawers, two pairs of woolen socks.

Our bedrolls have a rubberized backing, for sleeping in the wet and cold. We each have a mucket—a combination mug and small bucket. A mucket has a handle on the side and another on the lid.

Everything has USA stamped on it, even the soap.

Charlie calls out, "Aren't we going to shoot at the Rebs?"

"Weapons and ammunition are waiting for us at Camp Fuller," Sergeant Onley Andrus replies. "Company G, this car! All aboard."

Charlie and I board a train heading south for De Kalb County, in central Illinois. It's hurry up and wait again. We don't budge from Belvidere station for hours. Soon everyone is complaining about the hot wool uniforms. But no one seems to notice that, with my extra layer of clothes, I'm sweating buckets.

As the engine whistles, families and sweethearts seem to come out of nowhere to wave goodbye. The men rush to the windows, straining to see loved ones. Of course, no one has come to town to say goodbye to me.

The train finally leaves the station amid a flurry of steam, pocket squares, and tears. The First Methodist of Belvidere's choir sings "The Battle Hymn of the Republic": "His truth is marching on."

Mess sergeants hand around paper sacks of hardtack and salted beef for an early dinner. I've heard about this hardtack. It's like sliced bread that has been left out to dry for days and days. We wash it down with water.

"We're leaving Boone County in a few minutes," someone announces, and I look out the window at the Cleary farm, as flat on the horizon as sheets of green pond water. The sturdy barn and silo are the size of Christmas toys. I look closer. There're all five Clearys! They're standing next to the tree line where their farm ends. Each is waving a red or white or blue cloth as our troop train chugs past.

We drill constantly. We learn to snap open the stock of a Sharps & Hankins carbine repeating rifle to load and reload it. We learn to thrust our bayonets into hay bales. We learn to stay in formation during a charge. We learn how to pack our haversacks. We march for miles and miles to build up our strength. Then we drill some more.

These farm boys have been around guns since they could walk, and they sail through shooting practice on the first day. I have to train and train. I've learned to fold my extra towel against my right shoulder, for the rifle's recoil feels like it could break my collarbone.

"Private Cashier!" Sergeant Onley Andrus barks. He pulls my towel off my shoulder and throws it in the mud. "You planning to take a bath during battle, Private?"

"No, sir."

Sergeant Andrus puts his face inches from mine and gives me a hard stare. I will never, never use a towel as a cushion again, no matter how sore my shoulder is!

"Pick up that towel and wash it, Private. Then ten laps around camp."

"Yes, sir."

My entrenching tool has become a good friend. Lots of men go into the woods to answer calls of nature. I'm not the only one.

In October my monthly visitations stop.

Is there something wrong with me? Am I sick? There is no one on the face of the earth I can talk to about it, either. Then I remember Mr. Cleary once telling me that mares training for the racetrack become "racy." That is, they gain so much muscle and lose so much fat that they lose their monthly visitations, too.

Farm work turned my body to hard muscle. Constant drilling has made my body harder still. I've become racy—thank God for that.

Every six weeks I stand in line to get my regulation haircut, just as everyone else does. The 95th is mostly young fellows; some of us aren't shaving yet.

Having been in men's company for years, I couldn't blush demurely in response to these soldiers' raw jokes and ribald stories if my life depended on it. Except for my trips to the woods, and my constant companion, there are entire days when, I'm surprised to say, I forget I'm female.

Then there are days when I can't forget. Like the hot Indian summer day when, after a long hike, the 95th throw off their clothes and jump into the creek.

"C'mon in, Albert!" Charlie yells. "The water's fine."

"I . . . I'm wanted for more target practice." I retreat quickly. Two hundred ninety-nine naked men!

Everyone comes to supper cool, refreshed, and smelling considerably better. Everyone but me. The South is famous for its heat, but no matter how hot it gets, I'll never be able to swim with the fellows.

Charlie and I get to be good friends with Robert Horan, who becomes our tent mate. Robbie studied English Literature and scrivenering at Oberlin College in Ohio. He now works as the officers' aide de camp and secretary, writing dispatches in a clear hand. He boasts about fixing the officers' grammar, too.

The autumn rains turn Camp Fuller to muck. Our socks don't dry. At the first freeze the ground hardens into ankle-twisting ruts as we drill and drill. Half our company is off their feet. The other half is limping.

On November 4, Illinois Adjutant General Fuller comes to visit his camp.

Colonel Church orders us to fall into ranks,

stand in formation, and wait. Something is up—
something big. The camp rumors have been blowing hard on the wind all week. Some say we're to be
sent east to Maryland, to try to push General Lee's
Army of Northern Virginia into southern Virginia.
Others claim we're to be sent south to Corinth,
Mississippi, to stop General Van Dorn, who's been
trying to retake the town since summer. I've also
heard we're to be sent west to the New Mexico territory, to join Union troops from California, who
have been fighting the Rebs and their allies, the
Navaho. Or we may go north and out of the war al-
together, to protect Norwegian settlers in Hutchin-
son, Minnesota, from the Sioux.

If I had my druthers, I'd fight the Rebs: A colleen
from Belfast has no quarrel with the Navaho or the
Sioux.

General Fuller sits astride a magnificent gray
Percheron. I doubt General Lee's mount, Traveler, is
so stalwart. The general tells us we're to ship down
the Illinois River to the Mississippi River, then
south to Columbus, Kentucky. We're to serve under
another Illinoisan, Major General Ulysses Simpson
Grant, Department and Army of the Tennessee
River.

As we break camp, Robbie tells us what Sergeant
Andrus thinks of Major General Grant. "He says
Grant doesn't care how many men die under him as
long as the battle is won. At Shiloh he left wounded
men by the thousands in the field rather than surrender. For three days those men died, without

water or food, without doctors, bandages, or medicine. Can you imagine hearing them call for water, more and more feeble by the hour? Still Grant wouldn't surrender and allow the hospital stretchers out onto the field."

I say, "The Rebs gave up first. We won at Shiloh."

"But at what price, Albert?"

Charlie says, "We'll earn that sixty-dollar bounty."

"Aye, and thirteen dollars a month besides." *What have I gotten myself into?*

"That's not all," Robbie says. "We're going to Vicksburg on the Mississippi River. Major General Grant's reputation took a beating at Shiloh. He's determined to take that town."

5

THE BLACK RIVER

———————

"LISTEN TO THIS, FELLAS." FRANK MOORE, who was Belvidere's schoolteacher, reads out loud from *The Belvidere Standard*:

"December 16, 1862—The Union force to which the 95th is attached has captured Rebel prisoners and deserters. These footsore and starving men have revealed General John Pemberton's plans and actions. Although the Rebel general's fortifications were well secured for an attack from the north, the direction Major General Ulysses S. Grant was coming from, Pemberton apparently discovered that General William Tecumseh Sherman was closing in from the west."

"What does all that rigamarole mean?" Isaac Pepper grumbles.

"We were trying to set a trap," Frank explains.

"My guess is, General Pemberton has moved his army east, toward Georgia."

The *Standard* that Frank's landlady sent him is months old, but it helps us keep track of the war. The officers don't tell us anything we don't absolutely have to know. Even then, they only tell us what to do, not why we're doing it. I knew more about how the war was going when I lived on Mr. Cleary's farm. He'd read us the war news after supper.

We break camp in Camp Fuller, march west, and ferry down the Mississippi to Cairo, Illinois, on the *Dakotah*. We turn onto the Ohio and land at Louisville, Kentucky, then march to Cynthiana, only to break camp again after a week. We board the Louisville & Nashville Railroad to Memphis, Tennessee, to set up another camp. We break camp again and board the Mississippi Central to the Jackson, Mississippi, train station, only to be sent back to Memphis again.

Why? No one tells us. It's hurry up and wait. No one tells us how it is we're on these railroads, either. We control them, apparently.

I've never been down south before. I have yet to see a Rebel or a slave. On the long train trips to Memphis, to Jackson, and back to Memphis, the small farms and towns are like pebbles scattered across squared-off fields as flat as parlor rugs. Where are all the plantations? Where are all the ladies in fine dresses and their princely gentlemen, their gracious living borne on the back of the black man? These parts of Tennessee and Mississippi remind me of Illinois.

One afternoon in Memphis I see Frank Moore and a crowd of others nose to nose to nose, a mere inch from the ground.

I peer over their heads just in time to catch Frank's eye as he's looking up and out over the horizon.

"Look at this, Albert. It's an *Isia isabella*."

"Isabelle who?"

"The woolly bear caterpillar. It hibernates in a cocoon all winter, then hatches into the tiger moth in the spring." Frank frowns at the endless expanse surrounding us. "Although where a woolly bear could attach a cocoon around here is beyond me. There's not a leafed-out tree for miles."

"I've heard that you can tell how cold the winter is to be by looking at its woolly fur," I reply.

Frank allows the caterpillar to crawl up his finger. "The fur's not as thick as in Illinois. Of course! It's not as cold around here. I wonder what woolly bears look like in Vicksburg? Short fur, like a velvet smoking jacket, I'll bet."

"Why do we have to go to Vicksburg?" Charlie asks. I, too, have wondered about this, and I look to Frank for his answer.

Frank allows the woolly bear to crawl off his finger. It clings to a sprig of prairie grass. He stands up and addresses the men as though he were back in his schoolhouse. "Once Vicksburg is in Union hands, the entire Mississippi River is ours. Johnny

Reb can't send any food or supplies from Arkansas, Louisiana, or Texas. Reb sympathizers in Kansas and Missouri will starve for company. None of those states can send brigades our way, either. That's good news for us."

Last spring, when I was still working on Mr. Cleary's farm, President Lincoln sent the navy's Admiral Farragut up the Mississippi to Vicksburg. For ten days the navy pounded the three-hundred-foot cliffs below the town with cannonballs and assorted artillery. But the cliffs were too high, and even the mighty Mississippi was too narrow for the ships to back up enough to get a straight shot. When the large ships ran aground and caught fire on the muddy riverbanks, Rebels shot the sailors as they tried to scramble to shore. The U.S. Navy watched off their sterns as Rebels and townspeople alike swarmed over the foundered ships like turkey buzzards, looking for anything they could use or sell.

After Christmas, General Sherman ran gunboats down the Mississippi from Cairo to try again. Regiments from Ohio, Missouri, downstate Illinois, and Iowa charged the slippery Chickasaw Bluffs, north of Vicksburg, day after day, only to be shot down by the Reb brigades dug in at the top of the cliff. Entire regiments were lost: Small towns in the Middle West lost every young man they had to the Chickasaw Bluffs.

Then the Union tried digging canals, to link Louisiana's Lake Providence to Moon Lake. If we could join up the oxbow lakes, then join them to the Mississippi River's western banks, maybe we could take the town that way? But the canals overflowed as the swamps and bayous filled with spring rain. We were up to our chests in cold, muddy water, day after day.

Now, in April, the 95th receives marching orders. By the time we cross the river again and march south to Abbeville, Mississippi, to pitch our tents and make camp, the Lake Providence and Moon Lake canals have been abandoned. Our uniforms dry out for the first time in weeks.

Vicksburg stands, proud against the rising Union tide.

We know that Robbie Horan can tell us the officers' plans almost before they know them themselves. An ever-growing crowd gathers around our tent to listen of an evening. I stand next to Frank Moore. I've never known anyone who knew so much, and who didn't make a prideful fuss about his knowledge.

"We're going to force our way down the Black River in mudskippers," Robbie announces. "The scouts say it's swampy and we'll have to chop our way through in some places. The Black runs just beside the Mississippi on the eastern flank. The Black is more floodplain than river.

"We're to stop at Grand Gulf," Robbie continues, "about twenty miles south of Vicksburg. From there we're to march north and take the town."

I ask, "And what will the Rebs be doing while we

chop our way through a swampy river, Robbie? There could be Johnnies in those swamps."

"There could be Johnnies, indeed. But Major General Grant has sent Colonel Grierson's cavalry on a wild goose chase. He'll have General Van Dorn and the Rebs chasing him all over Mississippi and this side of Louisiana. They'll be too busy to pay us mind."

"That's a good plan." With the tip of a bayonet, Frank draws the outlines of Mississippi and Louisiana in the mud. "There's wilderness here, and bayous there. If Grierson's cavalry can keep them guessing, we'll have a straight shot down the Black where it joins the Mississippi below Vicksburg."

"We'll still have to scale those Vicksburg and Chickasaw cliffs," I say softly. "Entire regiments were killed just after Christmas."

Frank studies his map. "What if we tried to take the town from the east? There's got to be farmsteads, fields, roads—something—heading into Vicksburg from that direction. We'll be on foot—not on the river. No more three-hundred-foot climbs with the Rebs shooting down at us, is my guess."

"But first we have to open the Black River," I say.

Frank looks right at me. He smiles and I smile back. "I imagine they don't call it the Black River for nothing."

We stomp Frank's map into the mud.

Our ten mudskippers are flat-bottomed boats, twenty feet long, ten feet wide, with the engines removed to keep our troop movements quiet. Whale oil is a better lubricant than coal oil, so a steam engine has its own smell, like rotten fish on a humid summer's day. But now they can't hear us *or* smell us.

Sergeant Andrus separates the 95th into four divisions. The scouts walk along both sides of the Black, looking for snipers. The choppers stand on the bows and hack down the interlocking tree branches, some hanging so low they could knock our caps off. The punters are at the sterns using long poles to push the mudskippers forward.

Then there are the shovelers, amidships. Robbie, Frank, Charlie, and I are among them. We've buttoned our jackets to the chin. We've tied one another's sleeves and cuffs with baling twine. The lucky few have their heads covered with cut-up cornmeal sacks, their caps tied down tightly on top.

As the choppers hack away at the cypresses, black willows, tupelos, and Spanish moss, vermin by the hundreds jump onto the deck. Spring floods have set the critters on as high a ground as they can find; the tangle of tree branches above our heads is their only refuge.

"Verrrrrrr-min!" Sergeant Andrus shouts. "Shovelers, attend!"

A shower of terrified animals—wide-eyed and snarling—lands on me. I shovel raccoons, opossums, rats, nutria, and squirrels onto the riverbanks. Next come snakes, scorpions, spiders the size of my hand, cockroaches the size of my thumb, and lizards. I've got lizards on my shoulders, and snakes and scorpions curling around my boots. Hissing cockroaches seep between the wooden planks in the hull. We prize them out with our shovels if we have a moment to spare.

"Get rid of that snake!" roars Frank. A Prussian immigrant named Werner picks up a thick, striped snake by the tail, its snow-white mouth open to strike. He flings it overboard; it knifes into the syrupy black water with no splash.

"That was a cottonmouth," Frank says, his voice shaking. "*Agkistrodon piscivorus*. Poisonous. It'll kill you in minutes. Never pick up that species of snake by the tail! Do you understand me, son?"

Werner turns almost as white as the cotton-mouth's throat.

"Verrrrr-min!" a chopper yells down the bow. "Shovelers, attend!"

An opossum and her family land at my feet. Her babies are no bigger than newborn kittens. I scoop them all up and slide them gently off the deck. As they land on the riverbank, the babies scramble up their mother's sides and onto her back again. She glares at me, bares her teeth, and hisses. She creeps into the thick brush and disappears instantly.

"Another cottonmouth!" Werner shouts. "*Ach-tung! Achtung!*"

As everyone else is trying to shoo the cotton-mouth off the deck, a great brown spider, hairy legs and all, lands on my sleeve. Spider babies burst from her back and onto my coat, my face, my neck.

I can't help myself. I scream, "Get them off me! Get them off me!"

In an instant I'm thinking, *Lower your voice! Don't sound like a girl!*

Frank pulls his split cornmeal sack off his head. The mama spider rears up on her hind legs, ready to attack. In a flash, Frank wraps the sack around his hand and brushes her and her babies onto the deck. We grind them onto the hull. The spider babies were the size and color of new pennies. Their mother was the size of a man's hand.

"How many young ones were there, do you think?" he asks with a grin. "Fifty strong?"

"Not that many," I say, my voice pitched as low as Black River mud. Yet my heart pounds against my constant companion.

"Verrrr-min!" Sergeant Andrus shouts. "Shovelers, attend!"

"Albert, if you've had enough—"

"I'm fine." I brandish my shovel as though it were my carbine rifle.

"At least wear this." He whips my cap off and drapes the cornmeal sack over my head. I push my cap back on, and for the first time it actually fits.

At twilight the punters push us toward the eastern banks of a clearing. Sergeant Andrus shouts, "Shovelers amidships! Scour the decks. We're sleeping on the mudskippers tonight." We shovelers circle the deck once more, catching the smaller critters that had the pluck and good fortune to hide.

After supper we linger at our campfires. Apparently, I'm not the only one too jittery to sleep. Frank sits down beside me. I find myself wishing my hands weren't so filthy and that my face weren't a mass of cuts and scrapes.

Frank has black hair, tied back in the manner of a soldier from one hundred years ago. Even in firelight his eyes glow greenish blue. I feel safe with him sitting next to me.

"I never thought I'd see a Therophosidan arachnid on this side of the Mississippi River," he says. "I wonder how she got here—maybe on a floating log or a raft? Some jetsam maybe? Flotsam?"

"Theodore who?"

"That spider was a tarantula. They're not poisonous like cottonmouths, but a bite could make you sick for weeks. They like the Great American Desert, not in the bayous of Mississippi."

"I've never liked spiders. We don't have them that big in Ireland."

"Or northern Illinois."

I laugh.

"The females are a lot bigger than the males. I didn't know that Therophosidans carry their young on their backs, like wolf spiders. You were scared, weren't you?"

He said this not as a jeer or in a way that was meant to get my blood up. He sounded like a teacher stating a fact worth knowing.

I change the subject. "I've been wanting to ask you—how do you know so much? You know about state boundaries, and rivers, and animals, and history, and geography. And strategy. You think like a general."

"Reading," Frank replies. "The University of Pennsylvania has the biggest library in North America. When I was a college student, I spent every free moment I had in the library."

"You went to college? You sound American-born, too, but you can't be, not with a good Irish name like Moore."

"I am American-born. My great-grandfather was sent here to fight in the Revolution. In an American prisoner-of-war camp the guards talked him into fighting for their side. He never looked back."

I stare at Frank in amazement. He certainly looks Irish. But never before have I met an American-born Irish soldier.

"Why haven't I seen you in my school, Albert?"

I sigh. "I left school when I left Belfast. I had to make a living in America."

"You must have landed in either New York or Boston."

"The bishop told us to go to Queens, my brother and me—" I gasp. I haven't spoken of Tom Hodgers since leaving New York. I haven't seen or heard from him since fleeing the O'Banions' All Souls' Day table. His angry, jeering face seems to rise up in front of me, as red hot as the flames in our campfire. In my eagerness to talk to Frank, I've forgotten to be wary.

"Is your brother in the army, too? A New York State regiment?"

"I don't know," I say shortly. "We don't get on, Tom and I."

"Your parents?"

"They died in Ireland."

"You're in America all by yourself, then?" he asks gently.

"The families I've worked for . . . they're like family."

"I never see you writing to anyone."

"Black River coffee," Charlie interrupts. He passes the pot around, and we all pour slugs of the muddy brew into our muckets.

"Who's first going back on deck tonight?" Robbie asks us. "The U.S.S. *Swamp Crawlers.* Yowl! How they bite!"

"I am." I jump to my feet.

"Lamps out in fifteen minutes!" Sergeant Andrus says, loud enough for all to hear. "Pickets, take the line until two A.M. You'll be relieved then. Sleepers, back on deck."

A bucket brigade forms from the Black to dowse our campfires. We scatter into the woods with our entrenching tools, then make our way back to the mudskippers by starlight.

I slip into my bedroll and tuck it around me. Frank has not asked for his sackcloth back. I wrap it around my head.

"Look at Albert," I hear Robbie whisper. "He looks like a mummy."

"Albert's smart," Frank whispers back. "The rest of us will be bitten clean through by morning."

Thanks, Frank. Thanks for defending me.

"Do you want your sackcloth back, Frank?"

"You can have it. Good night, Albert."

"Good night."

I'm exhausted, but I don't get much sleep this night, perhaps because of the coffee before lights out, perhaps because of the near miss with the tarantula family. How many critters did we leave on board? How many will crawl on me before daybreak?

Jennie—what's gotten into you? You've never given in to girlish squeamishness before.

My mind races, but I don't dare twist and turn, for we are packed together like pickles in a barrel. One by one, the men around me go quiet, then snore. Frank's long body is beside mine. The rhythm of his breathing eventually lulls me to sleep.

The next morning we shift jobs. Punters go to the bow to hack branches. Shovelers go to the stern to punt the mudskippers through the water. The hackers are now shovelers, amidships.

We punters get a long look at the animals this time, for it's a good three or four minutes before the last of them are shoveled over the gunwales after each onslaught.

"Verrr-min!" Sergeant Andrus shouts. "Shovelers, attend!"

A wave of fur, teeth, claws, and tails surmounts the top of the mudskipper before crashing onto the deck. Shovelers work fiercely, and yet there are plenty of raccoons, opossums, lizards, snakes, spiders, and insects for us punters to scour off the stern with our boots.

"Look at that!" Frank calls out. He points to an animal about the size of a young pig but with a much smaller head. Wonder of wonders! It's wearing armor like the knights of old. "That's *Dasypus novemcinctus*. Let's catch it."

I put my boot out, and whatever it is bumps right into me. It rolls into a ball, as quick as a hand into a fist. I tap the gunmetal-gray shell. It feels like a turtle's shell. Frank pokes a finger between the metallic-looking bands of shell and feels its stomach.

"It's a mammal! Warm-blooded! Imagine that! My natural history professor told us armadillos are reptiles. I'll have to write him and set him straight."

"Armor—what?"

"This is an armadillo. It means 'little armored one' in Spanish. Those conquistadors were explorers, too, just like Lewis and Clark."

Gently, Frank tips the balled armadillo into the Black. It bobs to the surface like a sea scallop and paddles to the bank. It shakes itself off as though it has fur, then pig-trots away without even looking back at us.

"I've never seen such animals," I say. "It's another world down here."

"Fascinating. Endlessly fascinating. "

"Were armadillos on the Ark, do you suppose? Noah's Ark?"

Frank scratches his chin. "If Noah had seen a pair of armadillos, it seems to me he would have said something about them."

"Verrrr-min!" Sergeant Andrus shouts. "Shovelers, attend!"

6

EURIPIDES

---

*A*BOVE US, ON THE FIFTY-FOOT PROMON-
tory in front of Grand Gulf, ten long-legged artillery guns on stanchions are at the ready. They
look like giant tarantulas boiling out of the parapets, bristling for a fight. Some of the guns are
pointed right at us. Others are aimed at the river.
Others are pointed away, facing north. We're standing at attention in ranks a good hundred yards
downriver, too far away to see any Reb soldiers.

"Men," Lieutenant Colonel Humphrey says,
"there may be Rebs on those parapets. We won't
know until we're upon them.

"Your Sharps & Hankins stock-load carbine repeating rifles are the best rifles in the world. But
just because they're repeating, it doesn't mean you
keep shooting at nothing. Each box of ammunition

holds only four pounds of bullets. I know that seems like a lot, especially on a double-time march." A few of us chuckle in ranks. "I must warn you: Do not shoot until you see a Reb! Do not waste a shot. We are fighting this war in the enemy's territory, and we don't know where our next rounds are coming from. Wait for my signal.

"Company, fix bayonets."

We sharpened our bayonets on razor strops last evening. As one, all three hundred of us insert our bayonets into our rifles. The handles are turned to the right; the bayonets *clink* into place. A Sharps & Hankins rifle plus bayonet is taller than even the tallest among us. Mine is well over my head.

We're to charge the promontory and take it. There is no sound—none—coming from the parapets. All I hear is the *tromp, tromp, tromp* of three hundred pairs of boots along the riverbank—five in a row, sixty rows strong—marching ever closer to Grand Gulf.

Our first battle! My heart is pounding, pulsing blood through my temples. My neck throbs against my collar. The officers' horses are prancing, tossing their heads. Their nostrils flare. The whites of their eyes glow lividly against their brown coats. They must sense danger.

Don't show your fear. Fear will give you away in front of these men. All your training has prepared you for this battle. You can't falter.

I cast a quick glance at the soldiers around me. Their eyes bulge; their faces pale. Rifle stocks slip in sweaty palms. *The 95th is scared. Men get scared too,* I think with a shock.

At the base of the promontory, Lieutenant Colonel Humphrey raises his sword. Still no sound from the parapets; Grand Gulf is as silent as the grave. Is this an ambush? The only sound I hear is the mighty Mississippi, swollen with spring runoff, rushing past us to the Gulf of Mexico.

He drops his sword. "Charge!'

We scale the cliffs, silently skittering through the mud. I think about those men right after Christmas, shot down in waves as they ran up the Chickasaw Bluffs just north of Vicksburg. I'm careful to keep my bayoneted rifle well in front of me. I'm careful not to get too close to Charlie Ives's back, lest he be skewered by my bayonet. An artillery piece is pointing straight down at me.

Sixteen-millimeter. It could cut me to pieces! If I see someone, I'll shoot before he shoots me. No fear—

With a yelp, Charlie skids in the mud. He reaches out and clutches my hand for a moment. I'm careful not to step on him as we keep slipping and sliding up the cliff. My arms are so tired, I can barely hoist myself over the top.

Rebs! Rebs in gray uniforms! They're here!

Somebody starts shooting, and I start shooting, too. My bullets slam into gray clothes stuffed with straw.

Sergeant Andrus calls out, "Hold your fire! Hold it!"

All around us are dummy soldiers, dressed in

cast-off gray shirts and pants. We've been had. Our shots were a warning, but to whom?

I jerk my head to the right. Grand Gulf seems deserted—a few taverns, a cotton exchange, a grocery, a ladies' dress and hat shop—no one in the windows, no one on the riverfront. Captain Bush sends a scouting party around the perimeter and another to the town. The rest of us sit on the parapet and drink from our canteens—hurry up and wait.

"Sergeant Andrus," I say, "these aren't even real uniforms. They're just work shirts and pants dyed gray. They can't spare real soldiers here. They can't spare real uniforms, either."

"Good observation, Private Cashier."

"Sergeant, look at this." Charlie easily pushes an artillery gun off the parapet. It's made of cheap pinewood, painted black. Already the paint is peeling.

"They can't spare real artillery, either," Robbie says.

Maybe the Rebs at Vicksburg are dummy soldiers, too.

Our soldiers return slowly, with an old black man among them barely able to keep up. He looks scared to death. We all stare in amazement at a slave, a man who belongs to another man as though he were a steer, a mule, or a pullet. His civilian clothes are dyed gray.

"Captain Bush," Frank says, "this man knows the way to Vicksburg. Says he's been there a hundred times."

The man stoops a little and bows his head toward Captain Bush.

"How far away are we?" our captain barks at him.

"Afternoon's walk, sir." He has an old man's cracking, querulous voice.

"An afternoon's walk? Aren't we twenty miles south of Vicksburg?"

"Yassir, if'n you follow th' banks—they meander some. It ten mile overland to Vicksburg."

"Overland?" Captain Bush looks upriver, lost in thought. He turns to the old man again and his gaze hardens. "Anything we should know about going overland?"

The old man looks surprised. Maybe no one has ever asked his opinion before. "Don't follow the bayous. Look for the Indianola Road, 'bout a mile inland on dry ground. An' them gators's plentiful in the bayous. And hongry."

Captain Bush's eyes widen. "Alligators?"

"Yassir. Stay inland. You'll see th' big houses, but th' folks is gone. Run oft th' countryside, mostly."

"Civilians have fled their homes? Good. Where's General Pemberton?"

"I hear he in Jackson."

"What are you doing here? Is there anyone else in Grand Gulf?" Captain Bush softens his tone. "What's your name?"

"Euripides. Marse set me here to guard th' rice crop. Everyone else run oft . . . hide in country."

"Euripides, is it? We need a scout. We'll pay you two dollars a mile in United States currency to take us to Vicksburg. That's at least twenty dollars. Plus anything you can forage along the way."

Euripides's spine seems to straighten up as he thinks. "Yassir."

"Men!" Captain Bush shouts. "Commence foraging! Any cotton, we burn! Their ammunition is worthless to us; burn it! Any livestock and sundry foodstuffs we find along the way now belong to the Grand Army of the Republic, Department of the Ohio and the Tennessee!"

The men cheer.

Lieutenant Colonel Humphrey says, "Mr. Euripides, if you could show us that rice crop?"

For days we've been eating as though we were railroad and timber barons—three good meals a day, too: fresh roast pork, fresh roast beef, chickens, turkeys, butter, eggs, milk, peppercorns, cloves, blackberry jam, English marmalade, French brandy, fresh bread, jars of watermelon pickles, and spring rice and vegetables. We chase our food down grandly with Havana cigars.

Euripides showed us how to approach a plantation from the rear, then ransack the larder for food. He taught us to look for livestock in the woods and butter and silver in the wells. Everything we touch, we burn or take with us.

Even in Ireland I'd heard of these plantations, and all the stories are true. Surely not even Catherine the Great of Russia in her Summer Palace near Saint Petersburg lived in such splendor. The big houses are sprawling mansions, whitewashed mostly, with deep porches on the south and west sides to keep out the afternoon and evening sun. The ceilings are vaulted to trap the hot, humid air way above our heads. Grand pianos and harps, long tables polished to a deep gloss, and overstuffed sofas and chairs grace the cool, quiet rooms.

The windows are opened for the rare Gulf breezes, and heavy Irish lace curtains keep out the insects.

We ask Euripides about burning the slave quarters, and he says, "Burn it all." We burn the big houses and the quarters, too.

On our zigzag march to Vicksburg, for every one of these grand plantations we see maybe twenty one-room shacks made of raw wood. Each shack sits on a narrow skirt of land. We find out in a hurry that the plunder on these wee farms is meager indeed—a few ears of last year's corn, a few tobacco plants. We leave them alone. There're no folks in these shacks, either.

Why have these poor crofters left their fields and families to fight and die for the rich plantation owners? Why are the many fighting to protect the wealth of a few? It makes no sense.

We tell ourselves that foraging and burning will make the war end faster. When the women and their children return to these plantations and find their food gone, their barns, crops, and homes burned, and their treasures scattered across the county, they'll write to their husbands and fathers, asking them to come home. Their men will feel awful—unable to feed and protect their families. They'll want to come home to protect the very hearths they've gone off to fight for.

That's what we tell ourselves. That's how we would feel, were the Rebs in northern Illinois.

At first, the 95th ransacked the big houses for treasures and suchlike. But large booty slows us down and makes the march hotter. Now we scatter treasure to the four winds. A long trail of golden candelabras and punch bowls, silk dresses, feather beds, Persian rugs, mahogany tea chests, ivory fans, French brocades, English bone china, Austrian crystal goblets, and heavy German silverware lies abandoned in ditches and fields.

We keep the jewelry. The men line their pockets with diamond necklaces and pearl brooches to take home to their wives and sweethearts.

Euripides has taught us to tap on the walls of the bedrooms: A hollow *tock* means a lady's jewelry chest hidden between the rooms. He showed us how to look for a hairline fracture in the wallpaper and to push open the secret doors.

In an upstairs lady's boudoir, decorated in peach and sea-foam green, we have found a secret door. "Albert, look at this," Frank whispers, although there is no one but us in the room.

He holds up a three-strand necklace of dark gray opaque beads, each one so shiny and smooth, so perfectly round, that I can see my tiny reflection looking back at me from every one.

"Marbles? Who would be wanting a necklace of marbles?"

"Oh, these aren't marbles." Frank's voice is filled with awe. "These are pearls—the rare black pearls of the South Pacific. The ancient Tahitians buried their kings and queens with them. How did a black pearl necklace end up in backwater Mississippi?"

Another soldier storms into the room. "What'ja find?"

"Jewelry. Here." Frank closes the hasp, then tosses him the chest. The man tucks it into his jacket and runs off.

"Here." Frank slips the black pearls into my hand. I drop the necklace into my pocket before I have to chance to think about it.

Our foraging slows us down. Euripides's afternoon's walk has already taken four days. We have so many cows, chickens, and pigs in front of our lines that Lieutenant Colonel Humphrey makes us shoo most of them back into the woods. Our haversacks are so stuffed with delicacies that we sink into the damp, sandy soil with each step.

On the fifth day runaway slaves appear out of nowhere and walk along behind us, as quiet as ghosts. Every time we stop to cook a meal, dark men and their thin families seem to step right out of the very air to watch us. They sniff at our cook smoke and won't meet our eyes. Colonel Church orders half the regiment to go into the woods after the livestock we've just let go, for now we have more mouths to feed. The runaway men step forward and volunteer to look for firewood. Their women volunteer to cook, and what wondrous cooks they are. We eat like kings.

Now we move even slower, on account of the runaway families. Their men want to know all the war news. They savor all our victories as though they were their own. Which they are, I reckon.

On the night of May 14 we're just finishing a meal of peppered pork, greens, and corn pudding when huge explosions to the east seem to rip open the soft black sky. The horizon above the tree line glows fiery red. Frank points out Venus, Mars, Orion, and the North Star—the first stars of the evening disappear into the smoky blue lightness.

"Look, look." Charlie shows me a scrap of newspaper. "Albert, it's so bright that you can read a newspaper!"

I glance at his newspaper. The *Standard*'s headlines are a rolling boil of vexations:

LeePushingintoMarylandIsPennsylvaniaNext?
ArmyofthePotomacHalted
WhereIsPemberton?
PresidentLincolnConfoundedasSecretaryof
TreasurySalmonP.ChaseResigns
StonewallJacksonDeadRebelsVowRevenge
RichmondCorinthChancellorsvilleChattanooga
PetersburgSharpsburg
PeopleofWashingtonandBaltimorePrepareforSiege
asJapaneseCloseNewEmbassy

VicksburgLynchburgSecondFredericksburg
Williamsburg . . .

"That's the town of Jackson, I'm guessing," Frank
says. "That means Pemberton couldn't hold it."

"Major General Grant must have ordered the
town burned," I shout over the explosions. "Those
blasts must be the ammunition arsenals."

"Listen to that roaring fire," Charlie says. "That
has to be cotton!"

"We've occupied the city of Jackson, fellas!"
Frank crows. "Not just the train station but the
whole dang town! Listen to that cannon, like distant thunder on a summer's day."

We lie down with the muffled roar of siege in
our ears. Frank leans up on his elbow. "Are you all
right?" he whispers. Why would he ask me such a
question? I turn away and pretend not to hear him.

The next afternoon we huddle around Robbie,
who's spent the morning reading dispatches and
writing responses for Lieutenant Colonel Humphrey and Colonel Church. Robbie stands tall. We
see a light in his eyes that we've not seen for a
month of Sundays. It's the light of good news.

"Major General Grant ordered Jackson burned.
It was General Sherman who ordered the rails
melted. They've been wrapping the rails around
trees and calling them Sherman's corkscrews."

We laugh and cheer.

"But that's not smart," Frank says.

"We're wrecking their railroad tracks. The Rebs

can't use them. How's that not smart?" Robbie demands.

"The Rebs can't use them, Robbie. But now neither can we."

"We can't guard the tracks," Robbie retorts.
"We'll need every man to take Vicksburg. You think
you can plan strategy better than General Sherman?"

Charlie steps between them. "Whoa! Save your
vinegar for the Rebs."

Robbie turns on his heel and stomps away.

At dusk we see the 34th Indiana marching double time through empty fields, heading north. Some
of our men call out. "We're the 95th Illinois. Where
you goin', the 34th?" They put their fingers to their
lips and shake their heads. We give them jars of
briar jam, squares of cornbread, and peppered pork.

"Much obliged. Good luck, the 95th." A flat Mid-
western voice juts out of the darkness, like a sharp
elbow poke in the ribs. The soldier's accent is as familiar to me now as pork chops and sauerkraut.

On the night of May 16, cannonballs scream
from what sounds like east of Vicksburg. Explosions and fires light up the sky again.

Companies march near our camp all night. Some
are heading east toward Jackson. Others are heading
north toward Vicksburg. Maybe the entire Armies
of the Ohio and the Tennessee are on the march. The
companies kick up so much dust, we can't see their
legs. They seem to float on the horizon like ghosts.

We always ask them where they're from, and

they always call back: the 48th Iowa; the 16th Minnesota; the 117th Ohio; the 11th Wisconsin; the 32nd Indiana; the 6th Michigan; the 23rd Western Tennessee; the 2nd Illinois artillery battery out of Chicago's South Side. That 2nd Illinois artillery battery is the toughest bunch of mugs as I've seen since Queens. If we were all South Side Chicago boys, this war would have ended yesterday.

No one sleeps. Even without the explosions, the regiments marching near our camp all night have made sleep impossible.

"The Battle of Champion Hill," Robbie tells us next morning. "We had to win that one, too. It was the 34th Indiana's turn in the bucket. We're next."

"Why were all those companies heading east and north last night?" Frank wants to know. "Where are Pemberton's men?" No one has an answer, not even Robbie.

It is so quiet, this afternoon of May 17. The rotten-egg smell of gunpowder blows away, and then a curiously dry smell, like burning clothes, fills my nostrils. "Euripides told the officers that's the smell of burning cotton bales," Robbie tells us. "Jackson fell, Champion Hill has fallen. There's nothing between us and Vicksburg now."

I put my hand into my pocket so the black pearls can slip against my fingers. They feel cool and calming, like rosary beads. I see them in my mind, the same dark gray as the skies over Belfast on a winter's afternoon. The same color as inside the cockleshells on the Island Magee, come to think of it.

For one fleeting moment I imagine the black pearls draped around my neck, and I smile. Wouldn't Frank be surprised?

I will not think about why Frank gave me this necklace. I will not think about why he hasn't looked me in the eye since then.

We'll be storming Vicksburg soon, maybe tomorrow, maybe the day after. I'm a soldier: I'm not scared. No more scared than any other soldier in the 95th.

7

THE SIEGE OF VICKSBURG

---

*T*HE 95TH STANDS TALL IN RANKS AND AT the ready on a bluff south of town. At long last we see what it is we've been training for these ten long months.

It's a pretty town. Vicksburg is perched on a three-hundred-foot bluff overlooking the Mississippi River. I can just make out one of the signs above a store: TILLMAN'S SADDLER AND HARNESS MANUFACTORY, STAPLES, GOODS, AND GROCERIES. High above on a hill behind Vicksburg is a courthouse with the Confederate flag flying proudly in the early-afternoon sunshine.

Frank says, "Lovely Corinthian columns. Just imagine the view from that courthouse, and the breeze. It must be beautiful at sunset. Judging from the white color, I'm guessing Vermont marble—"

"Quit your blather," Robbie says crossly. "You're not Belvidere's schoolteacher down here."

"I could spend the rest of my days listening to his blather," I reply hotly. "Frank knows a bit about everything."

Robbie scowls at us both.

"What time is it, Captain Bush?" Lieutenant Colonel Humphrey asks in a measured, theatrical tone.

Our captain studies his pocket watch. "One fifty-five in the afternoon on May nineteenth, 1863," Captain Bush answers slowly, giving great weight to each word. "You men remember that. These Vicksburg folks will never forget it."

It's so quiet, I hear the birds singing and the river riffling against the gunboats. A stiffening breeze sets all the flags, both Reb and Union, to snapping.

Vicksburg itself seems to be waiting, holding its breath.

"Fix bayonets!" Thousands of bayonets on thousands of rifles clank into place like the gears and toggles of a gigantic machine coming to life.

At two o'clock sharp a Union gunboat on the western riverbank sounds its steam whistle—long, loud blasts. A great rumble rises up from all around Vicksburg. The roaring of thousands of men, eager to fight, eager to get the fighting over with, drowns out the steam whistle. It's as though the only sound on earth is the howling of our soldiers, calling one another to battle.

We're on all sides. The Armies of the Tennessee and the Ohio surround Vicksburg like a noose. The roar of thousands of men stirs my blood, sets my heart to pounding.

The river narrows at Vicksburg. Across the river to the west is the tiny town of de Soto, Louisiana. Our battery companies fire cannon at Vicksburg. The cannonballs scream across the Mississippi and hit the town full force.

Boom! Kaboom! Boom! Boom! Boom!

Tillman's store splinters to pieces. It catches fire. Great flames shoot into the skies. There's that dry, hot smell again—burning cotton. Half the river-front is on fire and we haven't advanced so much as a foot in any direction.

"Double time! March!" Captain Bush shouts.

We climb another cliff and march to within sixty yards of Fort Beauregard, the Confederate defense on Vicksburg's south side.

All around Fort Beauregard are trenches. There're Rebs in those trenches. Their bayonets glint in the sun; their officers call out orders; their gray caps with men underneath hustle every which way.

They aren't dummies in dyed gray cloth this time. These are real soldiers.

Lieutenant Colonel Humphrey lowers his sword. "Charge!"

We charge to within fifty feet of the fort, then sprawl in the mud. Colonel Church shouts, "Fire at will!"

We fire at the trenches and redoubts for about

half an hour, the Rebs firing back at us the whole time. From the trenches come screams; so much grapeshot fires above our heads, it sounds like a beeline to a honey tree.

Then Colonel Church calls us to retreat. "Inch along! On the ground!" he yells. "Make way! Artillery forward!" We crawl backward a good ninety-five yards, the tips of our boots hanging over the cliff before he calls a halt.

The gunpowder smoke is so thick, I pull my collar up over my mouth and nose to keep from choking. My eyes water. Everyone else's eyes are watering too, so I let the tears wet my uniform. But I press my lips together to keep them from quirking into sobs.

Quickly the 16th Wisconsin artillery battery sets cannon into position just ahead of us. In short order they blow up the Reb trenches. Clouds of dirt, blood, splintered wood, and bodies tumble before us. We shoot the Rebs who get up and try to scramble back to Fort Beauregard. The gray smoke and the gray uniforms—it's hard to see them, but we keep shooting anyway. I shoot anything that moves.

I shoot four men inside of fifteen minutes. I don't think about it. The men lie between the trench and the fort. They don't move.

Once the trenches are smashed, Colonel Church urges us forward again. The 95th Illinois, the 77th Illinois, and the 21st Iowa inch along, gaining the hundred yards or so we lost earlier this afternoon. We crawl over the bodies of the Johnnies, some still moaning, some still moving, and some still cursing.

"Charge!"

We leap to our feet and follow Colonel Church and Lieutenant Colonel Humphrey. I run uphill toward the Rebels, but not so fast as to get ahead of my company. As I run, heart pounding, gasping for breath in the smoky air, I feel a peculiar sort of snapping, then a falling away inside my shirt. Something settles around my waist.

The pink ribbons on Mrs. Windermere's constant companion have finally torn asunder. I don't know whether to laugh or cry.

"Hug the ground!" Captain Bush yells. "Get down!"

Charlie, Frank, and I stretch out onto the ground, making ourselves as flat as possible, as grapeshot and minié balls whistle past our ears. Just above us are Rebels. I can smell their tobacco. I hear them loading grapeshot into their fowling pieces— it sounds like rain on a tin roof. I hear them swearing at us, swearing at our mothers, our sisters, Abraham Lincoln and Mary Todd Lincoln.

Colonel Church, Lieutenant Colonel Humphrey, and Captain Bush stand beside us. "Don't waste a bullet! Choose a target! Take aim! Fire!" they shout.

For months now I thought privates did all the work, took all the risks. In battle, though, everything changes. It's the officers who lead the charges. They're in the line of fire much more than we are.

More and more companies come forward. We

are so crammed together that I hardly have elbow-room to reload.

Through the thick smoke I see Rebels hightailing it out of the trench in front of us. They're running toward the fort.

Colonel Church stands before us, sword upright. If he makes us charge the fort, we'll die in waves, just like those men on the Chickasaw Bluffs.

"Charge—"

No!

"—into the last trench!" Colonel Church roars. "The last Reb trench!" Charlie, Frank, Robbie, and I jump into the abandoned trench. Another fifty or so men jump in with us.

For the rest of the afternoon, the two sides take potshots at one another. Neither side gains or retreats.

As I load and reload, I take great, deep drafts of air. I haven't breathed so deeply, so freely, since starting work at Albert O'Banion's Finest Groceries in Queens. I forgot what it felt like to fill my lungs with air. Despite the smoke and dust, it feels like Heaven.

At sunset Lieutenant Colonel Humphrey himself tells us to retreat to our camp. We crawl out of the trench and backward to the bluff. Once we reach the riverbank, we commence to march south. We have about a half mile to go; the skittish among us break into a run.

"March as soldiers," Sergeant Andrus barks at them. "We are not turning tail! We are alive to fight another day!"

Our drummer boys tap out a brisk tattoo. The skittish slow down, and we all march double time, our canteens clanking rhythmically against our thighs while the battle grinds on behind us.

Once in camp, the 95th turns as one to look at the siege. Battle flames redden the orange twilight. Gunboats boom and send cannonballs screaming across the Mississippi. The Vicksburg riverfront is smashed, every building on fire or smoldering. In the rockets' glare I see men scrambling or sliding down the bluffs, then running toward the river. All our companies are retreating.

The cooks have kept our food warm. Most of us eat standing up, watching the war. Then, at 1:59 in the morning, all is quiet again, as quiet as it was at 1:59 this afternoon.

We can turn the battle on or turn it off like a steam engine. It's our choosing—not theirs.

Colonel Bush sends scouts to take inventory. They come back with sorry news: both railroad redoubts, north and south of town, still fly Rebel flags. So do Fort Beauregard and the courthouse. We have not taken the town.

We sit around our campfires, too exhausted and stunned to talk. I gnaw hardtack I don't even taste before swallowing. I drink slugs of thick coffee to wash it down. Our campfire smoke rises and joins the smoke of the artillery. It rises farther still to join the drifting smoke of burning Vicksburg.

The gunpowder in my lungs feels like rivulets of fire. Tears stream down my face, but these are tears from the sting of gunpowder, not fear. Everyone has tears on his uniform, not just me.

About three o'clock maybe, Sergeant Andrus orders lights out. I lie down in my bedroll, but I don't see the stars—too much smoke.

I've killed at least four Johnnies today, probably more. I've crawled over wounded men as though they were bales of hay.

Perhaps it's my deep breathing that brings up memories: Misty, smoky Belfast rises up like a landscape painting before my eyes. I see again the cockles on the Island Magee. I feel a scratchy skirt against my bare legs. I hear Jip and Col yipping in circles around the sheep and smell the pure, soft air above the Whitehead Bramble. I feel in my palm the penny a day Bishop Bannock paid me with a twinkle in his eye, for we both knew I was but a girl.

Why am I thinking about Ireland? How did Jennie Margaret Hodgers, a colleen and a shepherd, find herself in the Battle of Vicksburg, in the Confederate state of Mississippi?

That lass is gone forever. She's shot four men, maybe more, and she'll never come back. Jennie Hodgers might as well be dead and buried.

Goodbye, Jennie.

On May 21 we try again to take Fort Beauregard, this time with thousands of men from dozens of companies. Captain Bush hands out something new: one hand grenade apiece. Mine looks like a pistol barrel with wings coming out the back.

"Pull the stopper out, then waste no time throwing it a good seventy-five feet away from you," Captain Bush tells us. "Never, never throw one with Union troops around you. Especially if I'm leading those troops."

Hans Kirchenbaum steps forward. Hans is our ace pitcher and right fielder for the Belvidere baseball club. "Captain," he says, "I'll use my pitching arm with those hand grenades. I can pitch them one hundred fifty feet, easy as pie. We won't have to advance our position."

Captain Bush nods and calls for volunteers to give Hans their grenades.

Hans takes off his Union coat, his army shirt. His long, thick arms and shoulders are as broad and brawny as barn beams. His limbs have already burst the coat sleeves and pant leg seams of his uniform.

We cheer as he limbers up—stretching his arms, rolling his shoulders, and rocking his head back and forth on a neck the size of a country ham.

"I'm pitching high flyers, boys!" he shouts. "No sinkers today!"

With a big grin he winds up for the pitch and with a practiced air, lobs a grenade a good one hundred fifty feet, way farther than any of us could throw it, smack dab in the middle of Fort Beauregard. We cheer as we hear it exploding within the fort. I stop cheering when I hear men wailing in pain and terror, but there are plenty of men in the 95th who shout *Huzzah* with every moan and scream.

Ten pitches, twenty—maybe one every two minutes. The Rebs on the parapets disappear. They must be too busy running for cover, and treating their wounded, to shoot back at us.

Twenty-three grenades lobbed dead center into Fort Beauregard and not one shot fired back.

"Good work, Private Kirchenbaum, but save that arm," Captain Bush tells him. "We'll need it tomorrow." Hans salutes and falls back into ranks.

Lieutenant Colonel Humphrey orders the attack. We race up the fort's earthworks yelling, "Boone County! Boone County! Boone County!"

What Confederates remain rise up as one to shoot us down. We are pinned halfway up the earthworks.

I lie prone in the broiling sun. There is nowhere to run, nowhere to escape. Grapeshot thuds into the ground all around me. Frank is next to me. He scoops up a little wall of earth in front of his head, a good twelve inches tall and twelve inches wide, as a protection and cover. I do the same. Now the Rebs can't see me. All we can do now is wait for nightfall.

"Hide your face from the sun, Albert," Frank says to me. "Vicksburg is in the same latitude as Marrakech, Morocco."

"Is that where we're to be fighting next, then?" I ask crossly.

"Morocco is in northern Africa. This sun is strong." His green-blue eyes twinkle as he grins at me. It feels good to look into his eyes once more. "Get some rest."

I rest my face on my folded arms. I force myself to take short, shallow breaths, or I'll breathe dirt into my mouth and nose. I can't stop thinking of my canteen at my waist. It's full and yet I can't get to it. I can't raise my head upright to drink from it. My head starts to hurt from the pounding sun and from a powerful thirst. The skin on my ears starts to burn. Sweat slips down my face, my back, my legs.

All around us are the sounds of cannon and rifles, the moans and screams of the wounded, the sharp-smelling clouds of gunpowder, and the sickening smell of blood, sort of like rust overlaid with sugar.

From just behind us Union artillery batteries fire cannon over our heads. The cannonballs tear holes into Fort Beauregard. I wonder about those Johnny Rebs in the fort. What are they thinking? Surely some of them have received letters from their wives already. *Our food is gone. Our home is burned. When are you coming home to plow the fields?*

Surely the Johnnies want this war to end as fast as we do.

Maybe that's why they fight harder. For hours and hours it seems there is no halt to their fire. Again we don't take Fort Beauregard.

Colonel Church gives us the retreat just after dusk. Flares rocket into the air above Vicksburg. The flares will let us see how much damage we've done. We crawl backward until we're in a line of trees, then I—at last—take a long pull at my canteen. As I hunker down and sort of scuttle down the

94

earthwork, the flares light up our steps, Frank's and mine. We pass the bodies of farm boys from north-west Illinois, including the broken and mangled body of Hans Kirchenbaum.

Back in camp the runaways have fires lit and suppers cooked. There are fewer of us now, but Robbie, Frank, Charlie, and I are still alive.

That night Robbie comes back from the officers' tents, where he has spent the evening composing dispatches. Underneath the grit and smudge of bat-tle his face is chalk white. "Hans wasn't the only one who died today. Lieutenant Colonel Humphrey is dead, too. Captain Bush has ordered his coffin."

"He led our charge," I say. "How can he be dead? How are we going to know what to do without him?"

At once I understand: This is why officers stick together in their tents like a pile of thistles under burlap. This is why they attend those nightly meet-ings. If one dies, the others know his intentions and will follow them through. They will know what Lieutenant Colonel Humphrey would have wanted us to do.

We sleep uneasily this night. It was Lieutenant Colonel Humphrey who talked the Boone County Board of Supervisors into the sixty-dollar bounty for each of us. In the peace Thomas Humphrey was a lawyer. I used to see the shingle sign in his win-dow every time I went into town.

He and his eight sons marched in the Fourth of July parade every year. His wife packed enormous baskets for the picnics later in the day. After the fried chicken, cornbread, and cherry pies were eaten, his sons used to climb the oaks around the town square as the dignitaries speechified for hours on end.

How those boys would laugh as they raced to the tops of the trees.

The next morning after breakfast, we stand in formation with heavy hearts. Vicksburg has cost us plenty—seven dead and fifty-four wounded during the first siege, another eighteen killed and eighty-three wounded during the second. That's three hundred men down to a brave one hundred thirty-eight. And now this: Thomas Humphrey is dead.

Captain Bush stands in front of us. "Men, there's bad intelligence and good intelligence. There's no way of knowing which is which until time sorts out the difference." He nods his head toward the officers' tents. Our drummer boys beat a mournful tattoo.

Eight privates come out of the nearest tent with a coffin hoisted on their shoulders. Colonel Church holds up his hand: Our drummer boys stop.

There is no sound as the coffin is carried before us.

Captain Bush says, "Men of the 95th Illinois Infantry, I give you Lieutenant Colonel Thomas Humphrey." And Lieutenant Colonel Humphrey sits right up in his coffin. Robbie Horan gasps and turns white.

"Rumors of my death were needlessly exaggerated!" Lieutenant Colonel Humphrey shouts. We yell back in good cheer, shock, and relief.

The grinning privates lower the coffin to the ground. He leaps out and raises his hands to silence us. "Just like most of you, I spent yesterday pinned down by enemy fire. I was so close to Fort Beauregard, I couldn't leave until well after nightfall. You should have seen the faces of your officers about two-thirty this morning. It was as if they were gazing upon the ghost of Hamlet's father."

Here he gets a few chuckles from us, and a few sheepish grins from our captains, sergeants, and second lieutenants.

"We received a dispatch at dawn from Major General Grant. I quote: 'The enemy are now undoubtedly in our grasp. The fall of Vicksburg and the capture of the garrisons can only be a question of time. As long as we hold our positions, the enemy is limited in supplies of food, men, and munitions of war to what they have on hand. We'll have to dig ourselves in.'

"That is all."

DIGGING

AFTER THREE DAYS' REST AND NINE GOOD meals, we pick up our entrenching tools and commence to dig. Digging one long trench around Vicksburg is hard, sweaty work in this heat. The sun beats down on my head like a hammer. My hands are as rough and callused as Mr. Cleary's hands. But I prefer digging to fighting. So does everyone else.

After ten days of digging a trench all around Vicksburg, Major General Grant's Army of the Tennessee and General Sherman's Army of the Ohio are now a twelve-mile ring around the town, one regiment deep all around the ring. What Rebs remain alive in Vicksburg must be running out of supplies. Nothing can get in or out without our leave.

Robbie tells us that all those troops we saw marching near our camp the night of Champion Hill are posted in a second ring around Vicksburg on the Indianola Road. The Rebel General Pemberton can call for reinforcements until the cows come home. No one will get through to help him.

Our navy controls the Mississippi north of town, and south of town as well.

For the rest of May we dig underneath Vicksburg. We dig, then blow our way through rock with explosives. Meanwhile, our artillery, across the river in de Soto, blasts away at the town. We counted them once—two hundred cannon are firing at Vicksburg pretty much all the time, nights included.

Our fortifications are trenches with crisscrossed logs on top for extra protection. We plug the open spots in the logs with sandbags filled with Mississippi mud. When those bags dry out, they're as hard as stone. I can run the trenches without stooping over. It reminds me of running through the corn rows back on Mr. Cleary's farm. Taller soldiers are obliged to hunch over at the waist.

We're dirty as hogs and infested with vermin. We haven't had our clothes or boots off in four weeks. Trying to stay clean is so utterly hopeless that no one bothers. There's hardly any good water to drink; our coffee tastes like mud laced with gunpowder. The Mississippi is slick with whale oil from all our gunships. My canteen smells like rotten fish.

I try to remember to slouch, since my constant

companion is no more. We're all so miserable, and I've lost so much weight, no one gives me a second glance.

On June 1 the storefronts on one of the back streets catch fire. We didn't do that. No Union troops or gunboats are within range. No artillery in de Soto can reach that far. The citizens are burning and looting their own town.

The Rebs are so close, we smell their bourbon rations when the wind is right. They gamble in card games and curse their bad luck.

Every evening Johnny Rebs stand in the parapets of Fort Beauregard and serenade the Union troops with war songs. They sing in fine voices and close harmonies. "You Can Never Win Us Back" is a favorite, as is "The Bonnie Blue Flag." Their way of showing us their opinions, I reckon.

One evening a fine baritone rises on the still air with a song I've not heard before. Company G listens intently. No one moves.

"'Oh Johnny, oh Johnny, I weep to see you go.
Let us join up together—no one will know.
My chest I've bound; I'll wear my cap down
  low.
Won't you let me come with you?'
'No, my love, no.'"

The words chill my blood. Surely these men can't suspect that there are women soldiers among them? Or is this a song about wishing it were true?

"'Oh Johnny, oh Johnny, your words I can't
   abide.
Let us fall in together an' fight side by side.
Kit and rifle I'll carry; my hair's been
   shorn away.
Won't you let me come with you?'
'Nay, my love, nay.'"

Oscar Vander Zee sighs sadly. As does Michael
McGill.

"'Oh Johnny, oh Johnny, don't be so impolite,
For I love you far better than all of mankind.
I love you far better than words can e'er
   express.
Won't you let me come with you?'
'Yes, my love, yes.'"

I steal glances at my fellow soldiers. Each is lost
in thought, perhaps thinking of a Belvidere sweetheart. We're dusty, dirty—our trench floor is an
ankle-deep, buzzing ooze of blood, torn flesh, and
flies. Reb sharpshooters are the stuff of legend
now—we live with our dead until the runaways
have a chance to bury them in the skulk of night.

Who would ever want his sweetheart here in
this trench? Who would ever want to see her living
like this?

Suddenly, Michael McGill calls out, "Don't sing
that one again!"

Other men shout in agreement.

There is silence on the parapet—as though Johnny Reb is thinking it over as well.

A drawl twangs out of the twilight. "For once we agree, Billy Yank!"

We never hear that song again.

The people of Vicksburg have taken to digging caves in the earth in front of their houses. The caves give them some protection from our artillery.

Vicksburg looks like a massive prairie-dog town.

While on picket duty one bright evening in early June, Sergeant Andrus lets me look through his spyglass.

"See there!" he says excitedly. "We've licked them, Private Cashier. What do you see? No, in the middle of town—just there."

It takes a while to get used to looking through the spyglass. All of a sudden women and children leap into view. They're so thin! And gray with fatigue and defeat. The children look as though they've long since given up crying. What good would tears do them?

The women and children are prying up the floorboards from a dependency—a smaller building on the property—and taking them inside their cave. The puckered floorboards are shiny black. Behind them are piles of white clapboard and smashed chimneys.

"They're . . . taking the floorboards up from their outhouses? Why would they be doing that, Sergeant?"

"Not outhouses, private. The privies are in the

back. Those are their smokehouses. We've licked them!"

"I'm not understanding you."

"It's the salt left over from years of smoking meat. There's no salt to be had in Vicksburg. Imagine—no salt in this heat! Those poor devils are going to be sucking on plank boards tonight to get at the salt. Poor devils."

I can't keep from staring at the children—they can't be more than seven or eight years old. All the innocent devilry of childhood has taken wing. They plod from the smokehouse to their cave like defeated old men.

I say before thinking, "My heart goes out to them."

"I feel sorry for these folks, too, the children especially." Sergeant Andrus looks at me sharply. "Don't lose sight of why these women and children suffer, Private Cashier. That fool Pemberton could have surrendered a year ago: all this suffering, and all for nothing."

"Yes, sir!" I snap to attention as Private Albert Cashier.

"As soon as Vicksburg falls, we'll open the granary ships. We've got vessels full of foodstuffs docked in Grand Gulf south of town. Did you know that?" Sergeant Andrus says softly, "Once Pemberton surrenders, these starving people will have all the food they need."

We build fascines so close to the town, I can hear people singing in their roofless churches on Sunday mornings and Wednesday evenings. They're hymning to God for deliverance.

A fascine is an aboveground tunnel made of wood. First we chopped down every tree in the vicinity. The soldiers from the Wisconsin and Minnesota lumber camps take to the work more than the rest of us. Five of those brawny lumberjack soldiers can fell a tree, chop it to size, and stack it along the fascine wall in ten minutes flat. It was the 95th's job to lay the roofline.

Our fascine looks like a giant snake winding its way to Vicksburg. We run through it to deliver supplies to the miners—gunpowder, black powder, and detonators mostly.

On the afternoon of June 25 we hear low, loud *booms* on the northeast side of the town. The mining engineers must have set detonators and hundreds of barrels of black powder under Vicksburg. Explosions thrum the earth under our feet like vibrating bowstrings. Solders and civilians shoot up into the air.

It surely won't be long now. It won't be long before we can feed these people and welcome them back. I remember what Mr. Cleary said that day I left his farm. We'll all have to try to forgive and forget.

On July 3 the 1st Wisconsin artillery battery fires away to distract the Rebs on what's left of their parapets. The explosives engineers pack barrels of black powder into a cave we dug right under Fort Beauregard.

BOOM!

Half the fort blows fifty feet into the air. We're standing on the riverbank, but we still run for cover as a shower of dirt, splintered planks, and body parts rains down on us.

On the morning of the Fourth of July a white flag flies out from what is left of Fort Beauregard. The main gate swings open.

"Hold your fire," Lieutenant Colonel Humphrey orders.

A man I take to be Lieutenant General Pemberton comes out of the fort and glares down the earthworks. I catch my breath, for here comes our very own Major General Ulysses Simpson Grant, Department and Army of the Tennessee, walking up to meet him. Grant, Pemberton, and a few other men stand under a stripling oak tree, its leaves and bark gray with ashes, about fifteen yards from Fort Beauregard's sally port.

Major General Grant is small, like me, and seemingly mild mannered. He looks tired yet relieved, as though a disagreeable job is over with at last.

Pemberton talks and talks. Major General Grant shakes his head sadly. The aides de camp and officers on both sides watch one another warily. The Rebs, on what's left of their parapets, watch too.

Pemberton stops talking. Major General Grant says a few words, then shakes his hand. General Pemberton looks angry enough to spit bullets.

Major General Grant and his aides turn as one and walk away from Fort Beauregard. We watch them march solemnly all the way to the river. His own son, thirteen-year-old Fred Grant, is on one of those gunboats, or so I've been told. He's come to Vicksburg to watch his da take the town.

After about five minutes of complete silence, every gunboat's steam whistle wails. We cheer as the white flag goes up Fort Beauregard's flagpole.

Captain Bush tells us that the 95th Illinois will be allowed to march through Vicksburg. We honored few are allowed to make our way to Vicksburg's courthouse on the highest hill.

The people of the town watch us march to the courthouse. I've never seen so many starving, haggard-looking people. Not here, I mean—not in America. The children look shrunken, their hair as dull as dried-out grass. Their mothers and grandmothers are covered in grime and gray with exhaustion. They don't even have the wherewithal to look resentful. They just stare at us, hollow-eyed, as we march by.

The sight is too much for one of our own, Corporal William MacLean. He has small fry back in Belvidere. He walks up to a woman with four skinny children all trying to hide among her dusty skirts.

"Why didn't you surrender sooner?" he demands. He gives her his hardtack and salted beef and runs back into formation before she can thank him.

The surrender is announced. We all cheer as the Stars and Bars is taken down from the courthouse flagpole. We all cheer louder as the Stars and Stripes shoots up the flagpole in its stead.

Just as Sergeant Andrus had promised, as soon as our flag goes up the flagpole as a signal, the granary boats sent up from Grand Gulf open their holds.

Every church, every store, every public building with a chimney and hearth still standing, is used as a kitchen. The 95th feed the starving fried eggs and bacon, cornbread, apples, carrots, turnips, pecan pie, flapjacks, side meat, with plenty of coffee or lemonade to wash everything down. There's milk for the children. It's a fine Fourth of July picnic.

"I didn't come all this way to be a cook and caterer's man," Oscar Vander Zee grumbles. Several others mutter in agreement.

We're in what's left of somebody's house, the front rooms blown away. Civilians are on the lawn, eating as though in a trance. We've found enough unbroken dishes to serve fifty people at once.

A child laughs. I look up in wonder, for I scarcely remember what a child's laugh sounds like. Her mother, perhaps a few years older than me, stands behind her son and daughter in the rations line. Their clothes are as dusty as old horse blankets, but their hair, faces, and hands are clean.

I stare at the little girl. She can't be more than five. Her eyes are light blue; her hair, the very color of marmalade, is tied back in a black satin bow.

She looks just like me at that age!

"This is for you, lass," I say, handing her a plate full of bacon and eggs, cornbread, pie, and a pretty red apple. She turns shyly away. Her brother's hand, as quick as a bird, pecks three slices of bacon off her plate.

"Boy!" I shout. "You'll not be taking your sister's bacon off her very plate. Give it back, boy!"

He stares at me, terrified. The bacon goes back where it belongs.

"Respect your sister, Tom." My voice is shaking.

"My name is Roland," the boy whispers.

I hand him a plate with the exact same amount of food as his sister's—two eggs, four slices of bacon, a square of cornbread, a slice of pecan pie, and an apple. "Be on your way, then."

Frank is watching, his brow frowning in puzzlement.

"He can always come back for more if he's still hungry." My heart is pounding. I take deep breaths to calm myself.

That evening a song is borne along on the purple twilight. The words seem to come out of the very air, or maybe out of the flames of hundreds of campfires, both blue and gray.

"The Battle of Vicksburg," to the melody of "Oh, Susanna," seems to have always been here, waiting for us.

"On Vicksburg's globes and bloody ground,
  A wounded soldier lay,
  His thoughts were on his happy home,
  Some thousand miles away.

"'Oh, comrades dear, come close to me,
  My heart's with you today,
  Come hear the words I have to send,
  Some thousand miles away.

"'An' when you meet my mother dear,
  Be careful how you speak,
  The cords of life are almost run.
  Her heart may be too weak.

"'An' there's another so dear to me,
  She's gentle as a fawn,
  She lives behind yon distant glow,
  Down by the murmurin' stream.'

"The blood fast trickled down his side,
  A tear stood in his eye,
  He sighed, 'I ne'er shall see thee more,
  Sweet maid, before I die.

"'Oh, comrades dear, come close my eyes,
  An' make my last cold bed,
  Before the mornin' sun shall rise
  I shall be numbered dead.'"

"Was it worth it, Frank? Do you think it was worth it?" I stare into the campfire. "General Grant called for nothing less than an unconditional sur-render. There's scarcely anything left of Vicksburg *to* surrender."

Frank thinks for a moment. "If the surrender

makes the war end sooner, then it was worth it."

"Aye," I say doubtfully. I hadn't noticed how low his voice is pitched, like the Mississippi as it murmurs over rocks along the shore.

Charlie Ives's voice is starting to change. It squeaks higher, then cracks lower. I decide to change my voice too. From now on I won't utter a word unless the pitch is as low as Frank's.

9

THE SIEGE OF NATCHEZ

ON JULY 8, THE NEWLY PROMOTED Colonel Humphrey gives us our orders. We're to march south of Grand Gulf and take the town of Natchez, Mississippi. Another siege! My heart sinks into my regulation boots. I can't do this again. I can't face more trenches, more battle lines, more death, and more starving, war-blighted children.

Mississippi in July is so hot, the sun beats down on my head like a hardwood plank. I've unbuttoned my Union blue wool (everyone else is in shirt-sleeves), and my thirst and craving for salt are a constant presence. I can't drink enough water, enough coffee. I can't eat enough salt pork or corned beef.

Even the smallest effort brings beads of sweat to my forehead.

It is almost a year since the three hundred of us got on that train to Camp Fuller. Not even half of us are left from the original 95th. One hundred ninety are either dead or wounded so badly that they've been sent to the hospitals in Memphis.

How many of us will die trying to take Natchez? Our army and navy spent eighteen months on the Vicksburg campaign, worrying at the town like a sore tooth. How many months will this siege take?

"We'll be in Natchez by Sunday," Frank says softly that evening.

"I can't be doing this anymore," I reply in my new, deep voice.

We're around a low campfire, enjoying the first cool of the day. Mosquitoes and fireflies skirl around burning plank wood. Their bodies glow like sparks from the shed firelight.

These planked two-by-fours were from somebody's home, or somebody's barn, or somebody's store. Cheap paint bubbles off the wood in a hiss of steamed turpentine. It makes my eyes and nose water.

"Why did all those men die, then, if we quit and run? They can't have died for nothing. It won't be much longer."

"You sound as though you're trying to convince yourself, Frank Moore."

We talk of ordinary things again, and that's a comfort. But we hold the Tahitian black pearls as a secret between us, as a mystery neither one wants to acknowledge. To speak of it would mean invading an undiscovered country.

I've learned that women soldiers are called "petticoat soldiers," and at least one has been found out. The May 8 edition of the New Orleans *Daily Picayune* printed a harrowing story about a girl who called herself Charlie. She couldn't bear to leave her sweetheart behind, so she cut her hair and joined the 14th Iowa with him. As her sex was soon discovered, according to the story, she shot herself through the heart on the parade ground with her beau's pistol.

It took until after Vicksburg for that copy of the *Daily Picayune* to reach us. In less than an afternoon everyone in the 95th knew about Charlie. Those trained in oratory read her story aloud, again and again. None of the orators could read the ending without his voice breaking. Those who can't read asked to hear the ending again, and again.

Oscar Vander Zee is one of the readers. "'The delicate innocence of womanhood,'" he orates, "'dashed forever in the male arena of war.'"

The men are quiet, sopping away tears in embarrassment. They make a big show of claiming the latrines are beyond usable to go into the woods to sob. Backs turned, the 95th wept together as each soldier wept alone.

Could it be a flood of patriotism, from their sudden understanding that females, too, love the Union enough to muster in? Or could it be the love between the sexes that touches them so?

Delicate innocence my foot! I've never met a woman who didn't know as much about life as a man. *I* know as much about life as a man. Charlie traveled from Iowa to New Orleans, bristling with weaponry and always conducting herself as a soldier. Surely she was as proud as I am now, fighting for a nation that has given me so much and has asked for so little in return.

I shed tears for Charlie too, for my own reason. I only wish I had been there to whisper in her ear about hospital detail. Rolled bandages make a hasty yet sturdy constant companion. Such knowledge might have saved Charlie's life and saved the Union another headstone.

What a terrible waste.

Unlike Charlie and me, women are dependent on men for their food, clothing, even the very roof over their heads. They pretend an innocence of the world to flatter a man's pride and vanity. The men, in turn, complain bitterly about female guile and deceit. How are women to behave otherwise? Not being able to earn her own way honorably is the very key to a woman's soul.

I am so weary of this war. I could turn myself in to Sergeant Andrus now, at this very moment. The temptation rises to the surface like a dumpling in a bubbling stew. That article in the *Daily Picayune* stated that petticoat soldiers who refuse to go home are given two choices—prison time or working as a nurse in the army hospitals. Nursing pays just room and board, instead of the thirteen dollars a month soldiers earn.

I've never tried my hand at nursing. I could

leave today. I'd have to forfeit my bounty and my back pay, but at least I wouldn't have to face another siege.

Michael and Oscar join our campfire. Oscar passes around a box of peppery gingersnaps he got from his mother. They all share their mothers' and sweethearts' baked goods with me, time and again.

My fellow soldiers don't have the luxury of deciding to go home. Surely they're as battle weary as I am, but that wouldn't stop the army from shooting them for desertion. They have to stay until their enlistment is finished. Then they'll be harried to reenlist until this cruel war is over.

Since I left Ireland, my secret has set me apart from everyone. I have to be too wary, too watchful, to form close ties, lest someone discover who I really am. I didn't appreciate what a wondrous thing it was to have no secret that holds folks at arm's length.

But I'd lay down my life for Frank, for Charlie, for Robbie, for Oscar, for Michael. They'd do the same for me. And aren't I closer to them than I was to my own family? Aren't I? Even with my secret?

I wait for the answer to rise up in my head, like a canteen glugging up with river water.

No. The truth of it is, soldiering has brought me close to them, but my secret has kept me apart from them. And—were I to quit today, where on earth could I go? I have no home. Belfast, Queens, Belvidere—I can't go back to any of them. I have no one, no one but these men.

"Fresh fish!" somebody yells.

New recruits sit down next to us. The fresh fish have filled in the ranks of the dead and wounded from our regiment. They look like children on a Sunday-school picnic—bright-eyed and eager. Surely we couldn't have looked that innocent a year ago.

None of us has the heart to tell them what to expect. They'll find out soon enough.

Some of our runaways have decided to stay in Vicksburg. The government has figured out a pay scheme for their labor. They'll chop this year's cotton and the navy will float it up the Mississippi, now that the river flows unimpeded. Congress will pay them once the cotton is auctioned in Cincinnati. While they wait, the runaways are fed the same rations we receive.

The young men among the runaways proudly wear the Union blue. Some fall in and march with the rest of us. Mostly, though, they drive our wagons.

Euripides has been promoted in the field. He's now Sergeant Euripides, in charge of the runaway soldiers and drivers. He can drive, shoot, and lead a charge with the best of them. Colonel Church says we're lucky to have him.

The march to Natchez takes three days. The navy can't even spare mudskippers to take us there. We have to slog through Mississippi mud as warm as blood. We're obliged to sleep with our heavy wool coats over our faces, lest the mosquitoes suck us dry.

Tramp, tramp, tramp . . .

Late morning on July 12 we march double time toward another pretty river town, with cannon, guns, and bayonets at the ready to destroy it. There are no trenches, no fortifications. No artillery, false or otherwise, points down at us from the levees. It's so quiet, even the Mississippi just murmurs by.

One old man stands alone on the levee in front of Natchez, watching us approach without so much as a twitch of alarm. His civilian clothes—a spotless white linen coat with crisp matching trousers—are well cut. His right hand holds a cane; his whole person leans against it. With his left hand he removes his Panama hat and transfers that hat to his right hand. He dabs a handkerchief on his forehead with elderly delicacy.

The heat blares white hot against the white-washed homes, stores, and churches. It hurts my eyes just to look at Natchez.

"Men, halt!" Captain Bush shouts. "Atten*tion*." We punch our rifle butts into the levee. A cloud of dust drifts north, toward Vicksburg.

The old man tips his cane to us. "How d' do, gentlemen?" he calls out. "I'm the mayor of Natchez. What can I do you for on such a fine morning?"

"You will surrender your town immediately, sir," Colonel Humphrey says.

The mayor looks startled. "Surrender to whom?"

"The Grand Army of the Republic, Department

and Army of the Tennessee," Colonel Humphrey replies.

The mayor takes his time looking us over. "Y'all from Tennessee?"

"No." Colonel Humphrey shifts a bit in his boots. "We're from Illinois, northwest of Chicago. We're the Department and Army of the Tennessee River."

"Chicago? So y'all aren't from that war back east?"

Colonel Humphrey looks taken aback. "Well, yes. Yes, we are."

"Well, sir, we in Natchez haven't paid any mind to that war. It's a business matter: All the planters here in the Homochitto Valley sell all their cotton to a Mr. Abraham Gratz of Pittsburgh, Pennsylvania. Y'all know Mr. Gratz?"

Colonel Humphrey opens his mouth to speak, then closes it again.

The mayor asks, "So how many soldiers are y'all?"

"Enough . . . enough to take your town," Colonel Church stammers.

"You misunderstand me, sir. A regiment is three hundred men, is that right? I reckon we've got enough ladies in town and in country to accommo-date you. They can put up two, three soldiers apiece." The mayor takes a timepiece out of his vest pocket. "Y'all are in luck—just in time for Sunday dinner."

Colonel Humphrey looks shocked. "We will not break up our regiment, sir. We are at war!"

"Well, now." Slowly, the mayor tucks his handkerchief and timepiece into his vest pocket. This time I detect the faintest tremor in his hand. *He's afraid and trying hard not to show it.*

While the mayor thinks, we stand at attention, sweat dripping off our chins. The heat rises in waves off the levee. Natchez looks to be dozing, nodding off in the noonday sun.

"Could y'all set up camp behind the First Methodist? The land slopes up to Mrs. Armstrong's pasture."

Our colonels shade their eyes toward a white steeple south of downtown. Behind it are deep shade trees and pasture grass riffling in a freshening breeze. "That would suit. Uh . . . thank you, Mr. Mayor. I'm Colonel Thomas Humphrey."

"I'm Colonel Edward Church."

"I'm Mayor John Hunter. Mind your step round the cow flops, colonels. Once settled, meet me front of the First Methodist. We'll keep Sunday dinner hot for you Chicagoans."

During the next week all but our runaways are invited to Sunday dinners, Tuesday-evening piano recitals, Thursday-afternoon card clubs, and Friday-evening fish fries. The foreign-born are asked to give little speeches in the town hall of an evening. The Austrians and Prussians among us speak of their childhoods under the hard reigns of the Habsburgs and the Romanovs. The Germans speak of living in a crazy quilt of shabby dukes and petty princes, each more demanding than the next. The rest of us speak of Ireland, and the Netherlands, and Norway.

We are praised for our parents' gumption in quitting Europe and for our proficiency in spoken English.

There are always lots of questions afterward as the ladies of Natchez pass plates of butter cookies and punch cups of tart lemonade.

On Saturday the ladies open their homes and insist that we stay with them. They declare themselves wretched and claim to toss and turn all night, thinking of us brave men on wet ground and so far from home.

Our officers look the other way as by twos or threes we leave the pasture and settle into balmy, shaded homes with more porches than rooms, with more outdoors to them than indoors. There are bathtubs and laundries, featherbeds, and palmetto fans.

Soon the 95th is repairing staircases, hoeing vegetable gardens, and chopping wood for summer kitchens. We whitewash houses, fences, and barns. We repair levees with the same Mississippi River mud we used to fortify our trenches back in Vicksburg.

The ladies of Natchez declare themselves grateful and much obliged, what with all their men gone and leaving them defenseless. We are coaxed onto porches during the worst heat of the day with frosted pitchers brimming with big chunks of ice and more lemonade.

Frank and I are staying with a Mrs. John Williams. It would never do to have a battle-hardened soldier admiring her flowers. So, when no one is looking, I stand under her magnolia tree on the shady side of the house. The leaves are holly dark, the last of the blossoms purest white. The blossoms smell sweet but with a crisp, lemony underscent, like butter cookies and tart lemonade.

On August 19 at a town barbecue, Colonel Church announces that we must march out tomorrow morning. The 95th groans, and the ladies of Natchez declare themselves heartbroken. With fans fluttering at their necks, they ask our colonels to please leave some of these brave men behind, to protect them against soldiers who might not be the gentlemen that we so obviously are.

We watch in amazement as Colonel Humphrey bows from the waist and promises the ladies fifty-five men to guard them. No, Colonel Church says, stepping forward—seventy-five men.

The mayor invites everyone back once this little misunderstanding is over. "Our doors remain open," he says, as the ladies murmur in agreement.

We march out at dawn. Someone has hung a banner on the town hall:

FAREWELL TO THE GALLANT GENTLEMEN
OF THE 95TH, BOONE COUNTY, ILLINOIS.
THE LADIES OF NATCHEZ THANK YOU!

The ladies press molasses cakes, sugar cane, and

pecan tarts into our hands. They wave lacy hand-kerchiefs and cry: "Y'all take care! Come back and see us soon."

We promise we will.

As we march away, their cries become fainter and more melancholy, like the piping of children called back to classes from their schoolyard. They seem genuinely sorry to see us go. But aren't we the enemy?

After our noon meal we're ordered back into ranks. Colonel Humphrey tells us we're to march up the Indianola Road (no foraging this time) and back to Vicksburg. The Johnnies we fought against have been sent upriver to Camp Douglas, a prisoner-of-war camp on Chicago's South Side. It's up to the 95th to mend the hearts and minds of Vicksburg.

The colonel hesitates. "I've thought long and hard about what happened in Natchez these last five weeks," he says. I listen closely, for I declare myself mystified.

"The men of the 95th were witness to that institution of song and story—Southern womanhood. Mayor Hunter knew all about Vicksburg. He knew we could have burned Natchez to the ground in less than an afternoon, what with their men off fighting. He knew all about our foraging in country.

"The fact is, he set upon us lonesome soldiers his secret weapon, and we were as helpless as newborn kittens before it. The ladies of Natchez charmed the fight right out of us. Companies, march!"

Robbie asks me at campfire this evening, "We're taking bets: which of the ladies of Natchez was the prettiest? I've got twenty dollars on Marazine Menard." Robbie sighs. "Didn't she look like a dancer on a music box?"

I say in my new, low voice, "I didn't think of the ladies that way."

Robbie snorts. Frank stares at me. "What's wrong with your voice?" he asks. "You sound like you're sick."

Sick?

"G'night," I say, getting up quickly. "G'night."

10

GUNTOWN

---

*T*HE 95TH HAS BEEN OUT OF THE FIGHT for six months now—not that anyone is complaining. Rebuilding Vicksburg, and feeding thousands of starving civilians from the surrounding countryside, has become a full-time job.

Rebuilding Vicksburg is hard work; I expect I'll be able to earn good money as a carpenter once this war is over. Or maybe I can be a cook in one of those fancy hotels on Michigan Avenue in Chicago.

It's our second Christmas in the army, and we're feeling lowdown. To cheer Frank up, I tell him a true story about the giant catfish we called The Big Murky that lived in Mr. Cleary's cow pond.

It was a hot day in August, three summers ago. The herd was udder-deep in the cow pond, their tails drifting on the surface of the muddy water.

The Big Murky grabbed the boss cow by the tail. Bossy leaped out of the pond, dragging the giant catfish behind her. She ran around the pasture bellowing, as the other cows lumbered out of the cow pond after her in dim, bovine panic. Bossy started to buck. Maybe she thought she could persuade The Big Murky to give up the fight. All the other cows commenced to buck too, although they didn't have catfish attached. The bucking cows reminded me of the line dancers with crowns of pink feathers in their hair at the Olympic Theatre in Manhattan.

After three good runs around the pasture, Bossy bucking and bellowing all the way, The Big Murky must have decided that he'd enough, for he let go. We rushed over to get a good look at him. He was the size of a six-year-old, his whiskers longer than a rifle barrel. The Big Murky's eyes had bugged out and he was panting hard, giving him a shocked yet thoughtful appearance.

Just as Mr. Cleary had called out, "We're having catfish tonight!" The Big Murky commenced to snake and skirr toward the cow pond. He was too slippery to catch with our bare hands. To my knowledge, he never bit a cow's tail again.

Frank laughs. He tells me about how the Chinese believe catfish know when an earthquake is coming. For this reason, catfish are revered as gods. Frank thinks their whiskers, so sensitive and low to the streambed, can sense the tremors of an earthquake before people begin to feel it.

Robbie walks by. What he says hisses out of him,

125

as soft as the tongue flick of a snake: "Couple of nancy boys."

Frank lunges up and tackles him. They roll in the mud, punching each other hard. It occurs to me that I should lunge up as well; surely my honor is as besmirched as Frank's.

Soldiers leap to their feet, form a circle around them, and chant, "Fight! Fight! Fight! Fight!" The men's eyes gleam in delight. They hit the air with their fists and cheer when either Frank or Robbie gets in a particularly good punch.

"Stop! Please stop!" I yell, but the chanting drowns me out.

It takes Sergeant Euripides and two corporals to pull them apart. The soldiers go back to their campfires, disappointed. Neither combatant will say what the fight was about. Francis Patrick Moore and Robert Charles Horan are ordered to spend the rest of Christmas Day, and the next ten days and nights, in the holds of separate gunboats.

Frank and I don't talk, or sit next to each other, for a month.

In April 1864 we are sent to northern Mississippi, to guard the west side of the Tombigbee River, just where it flows into Alabama. Now that the Mississippi River is blocked, the Rebs have been using the Tombigbee to send supplies and men south to Mobile and the Gulf of Mexico.

Major General Grant is with General Meade and the Army of the Potomac in Virginia. We have a new general. General Sturgis is a plump man, which we notice right away on account of food being so scarce. He's a Pennsylvanian, too, not that we hold it against him, but the fighting is different in the west. Out here we don't have the big battles, except for Vicksburg.

There aren't the big cities either. There weren't more than 3,400 civilians in Vicksburg during the siege, maybe half that in Natchez.

Northern Mississippi is cypress swamps, bayous, seepages, and bottomlands. The roads and farms are on high ground and sheltered by stands of longleaf pines. Any place you'd care to look, there could be Rebs hiding, waiting to make trouble. General Sturgis appears lost most of the time; Mississippi must look nothing like Pennsylvania.

He marches us far northwest of the Tombigbee and sits us in camp all spring near the tiny town of Stubbs Farm while his cavalry gallops hither and yon. The scouts ride back to camp with wild tales of vast armies of Confederates lying in wait, eager to restore their honor. General Nathaniel Bedford Forrest, a graduate of West Point Academy in New York State, and a man we've dreaded for all the trouble he's caused in western Tennessee, is spoiling for a fight.

Sturgis looks scareder and scareder, if that's a word, with each report. Maybe Grant had his undecided moments too, but he never showed us his fear. Knowing that our general is spooked does not sit well with the 95th or any of the other regiments at

Stubbs Farm. If he turns tail, how will he lead us? It has never before occurred to me—never—that we might be poorly led in this war.

Even Colonel Humphrey and Colonel Church look uneasy. In the heat of battle they will have to follow General Sturgis's orders and not their own judgment. To disobey orders is to end up in irons in a gunboat's hold, or worse.

Robbie comes back from the officers' tent late one afternoon in early June. "Sturgie has no idea of the number of Reb forces," he tells us in a voice so low that we must crowd around him shoulder to shoulder to hear him. "He thinks Forrest might be leading as many as forty thousand men."

Charlie snorts. "Forty thousand men? That's nonsense! There weren't half that many Rebs at Vicksburg."

"Colonel Humphrey thinks as you do," Robbie whispers.

"Forty thousand men," I repeat in amazement.

Frank is next to me. We haven't said much to each other since Christmas. He turns away without a word.

This evening Frank joins another campfire. I can hear him laughing from across the campground.

At seven the next morning we stand at attention on parade. Muttering to himself and shaking his head, General Sturgis shambles back and forth before us. Finally, he turns and speaks. "Men, it's impossible to gain any accurate or reliable information of the enemy. We've tried and we've failed."

His words are like a slap of cold water in an Illinois January. No officer has ever spoken to us like this, much less a general. His fears and doubts spread among us with the speed of a diphtheria contagion.

The rain stops at dawn. As the sun rises higher, the June sun beats down on our heads. It's humid, without a breath of a breeze. Swamp gas rises off the sluggish water and hangs suspended above the low country.

Even after more than a year in the Deep South, the 95th still isn't used to the heat. Men collapse from sunstroke all the time. This is definitely a sunstroke day, and it's still early yet.

General Sturgis dismisses us and sends his cavalry down the Ripley–Guntown Road with orders to scout the situation. We wait in an uneasy quiet for them to return. I keep my hands busy with the mundane while my mind races along on the immortal.

Our general thinks we're going to die today. I stare at every blade of sedge grass; the sunshine glints off the necks and withers of our horses; I burrow my feet into the shadiest part of the streambed and savor the coolness; the birdcall is cheerful, the bird feathers bright against the deep green of the trees.

Have I accomplished anything worth telling Saint Peter about, assuming I get to Heaven before the Devil knows I'm dead? Is this enough? Taking the time to wonder at how beautiful the world is before I leave it forever?

I haven't been to Mass, or taken communion, or gone to confession, in years, not since St. Brendan's in Queens. I've long since lost track of the days of the week, so my Friday abstinence is out the window as well. There's no fish to be had anyway—I eat salted beef or salted pork with every meal.

My lapses won't put me in good stead with the Lord, but what is a soldier in the field to do? There are no parishes in northern Mississippi. Even if there were, I doubt the parishioners would let me sit among them, much less pray for Union victory.

I slip my black pearls over my fingers and make myself look at the bad things I've done. Most of them have been because of my secret. I've hurt good people; they've received me warmly and in good faith, and I've lived as a lie among them. I've walked away from good folks because it was easier than being truthful.

And then there's Frank. Whatever it is we have, it's based on a lie.

I can't deny that God made me one way and I've taken it upon myself to be another. I can't believe He's indifferent to that. But I had to be Georgie Hodgers in those days. Tom and I were all alone in the world; we needed the money Georgie could bring us. Jennie could never have brought in so much money.

I whisper into the sultry, steaming air, "Lord, if

I survive this day, I'll make amends. Even if it takes the rest of my life, I'll make amends. If I have to start my life all over again, that will be my penance."

The officers let us linger over the breakfast washing up and our laundry. Since I can't swim with the others, I volunteer for laundry detail whenever I can. I can splash myself with water and no one is the wiser.

The sun rises higher: Maybe there won't be a battle today.

Before noon a rider comes back, his horse lathered and blown.

"They're at Bryce's Crossroads!" he shouts. "Major McMillen needs reinforcements! He says make all haste. Lose no time in coming up."

General Sturgis rushes out of his tent. "Where is Bryce's Crossroads?"

"The fighting is seven miles down the Ripley–Guntown Road, General. Where it meets the Wire Road on the bridge over Tishomingo Creek. Rebs are everywhere!"

As we grab weapons and ammunition boxes, and pull on boots, the rider leaps on a fresh horse and gallops toward the battle. His winded horse staggers over to the stream, sucks muddy water down her gullet. Charlie unbridles and unsaddles her. She lies down in the deep shade of a tupelo.

We march double time toward the Wire Road. The midday heat beats down stronger. My four-pound ammunition box is a dead weight in my haversack. On the far horizon telegraph-wire poles rise up in a line like rifle barrels emerging from a trench. That's the Wire Road, and we're marching closer to it with every step.

I can't sweat enough to cool down. My head starts to hurt, my legs to tremble—sure-fire warnings of sunstroke.

We hear the battle before we see it. Gunfire, hollering, horses screaming—the Rebel yell chills my blood despite the heat of the day.

For a good mile, horse-drawn wagons, artillery, and ambulances clog our way. We march; we walk; we mill about. Why are our supply companies in front of us? We've got a battle to join!

As we reach for our canteens, Captain Bush orders us to go around the wagons and toward the bridge. The embankments on either side of the Ripley–Guntown Road fall away to bogs and rice fields. Suddenly, there are Rebs running toward us! We slide down the embankment, lie flat in the mucky rice fields, and fire on them. They keep coming.

I watch in amazement as they run right past our lines without firing a shot. They ignore us—they don't even meet our eyes.

With whoops and hollers, the skinny Johnny Rebs scramble up the embankments. They shoot the drivers. They crack open the supply wagons. "Bacon! Billy Yank's got bacon!" Rebs whirl bacon slabs above their heads. They swarm over the wagons, downing hardtack and raw bacon. They lift their chins and let raw eggs slide down their throats. More starving Rebs clamber up the embankments behind them.

"Regiments! This way!" Major McMillen shouts at us. "To the bridge!"

We march through entire Rebel companies, neither side firing a shot. They don't even yell insults as they run by. Their eyes are on those wagons.

At the bridge our cavalry is dismounted, their horses fled. They're fighting hand to hand with Rebs who are trying to seize control of the Tishomingo Creek Bridge. As cannon fire, our wagon teams spook and drag their loads down the embankments. Rebs cut the traces with their bayonets. Terrified teams gallop off in every direction.

More Johnnies swarm over the wagons, trying to salvage payloads before they sink into the mire. The faster they pile on, the faster the wagons sink.

"Hams! Billy Yank's got hams!"

"Maple syrup!"

"Lard! Cornmeal!"

"God Almighty! Peaches! Billy Yank's got peaches!"

"The 95th into companies!" Captain Bush shouts. "Prepare to fire!"

I discover that it doesn't pay to stay in one place on this soft ground. The trick is to keep moving. Company G swarms back and forth shooting Rebs into the muck.

"Our cavalry line is broken!" General Sturgis shouts.

Just in time, Colonel Grierson's cavalry and the Minnesota and Indiana regiments appear at the bridge. To my astonishment the Confederate bugler blows the retreat. With their arms full of booty, Rebs race across the rice fields and into the dark woods.

Impossibly—the battle is over.

"Did we win, Frank? Can we retreat to Stubbs Farm?"

"It's early afternoon." Frank glances at the sun. "Albert," he says softly, "go back to Stubbs Farm without me."

"Wh-what do you mean?"

He grabs my arm. "They're going to come back, madder than ever, and bent on spoils. Our cavalry line is broken. Maybe there really are forty thousand men against us." His voice drops. "Forrest is a genius and Sturgie is a fool—we're going to lose. Badly. Go back to Stubbs Farm. It'll be safe there."

We regard each other for a moment. And another moment.

"Come back to Stubbs Farm with me," I say. "We'll both be safe."

"Check your ammunition!" Colonel Humphrey shouts. "The 14th Iowa Maintenance—bring ammunition from the rear!"

The 14th Iowa marches to the rear just as a double shot of canister roars out of the Reb cannon on both sides of the rice fields. Their bugler sounds the charge. Johnnies pour out of the forests, thousands

134

of them, shrilling the Rebel yell and firing their rifles. This time they're running toward us, not the wagons.

Colonel Church shouts, "Fire at will!"

Frank pulls me under the bridge. We duck behind a stanchion. I'm up to my armpits in the blood-warm Tishomingo Creek. We drink our canteens dry, then fire at Rebs who get close enough to the bridge for a good shot. When our ammunition is gone, Frank runs out onto the embankment and takes up the haversack of a dead soldier. We share his ammunition until it's gone. He runs out again and comes back with two Reb guns and ammunition this time.

It takes us a while to figure out how to load the weapons. "This musket is from the eighteenth century," Frank mutters, holding up a powder horn. "How can they be beating us?"

We take aim, shoot, but the Rebs don't go down. These muskets don't have the range of our carbines. We have to hold our fire and wait till the Rebs come closer.

By now I'm shivering from standing in water all afternoon. I can't hold my aim steady. The bloody Tishomingo is clogged with dead fish and crawdads. So many turtles have crawled out of the crimson water, the creek banks look like streets of cobblestones.

The sun is setting, blood red on the tree line. Union men now run at full tilt away from Guntown and toward Stubbs Farm. A retreat! They splash across the Tishomingo, holding their Sharps & Hankins rifles above their heads.

"Did you hear the retreat signal?" I ask Frank.

A boy splashes across the creek and runs right into me. "Soldier! What's the news at Guntown?" I ask him.

Our coats are off and the boy takes wild swings at me. "Whoa! Whoa! We're not Rebs." I hold up my blue jacket.

"Where are you from, son?" Frank asks in his best schoolteacher voice. Frank's voice—calming, friendly, yet full of authority—makes the boy's breathing come a little easier.

"Dubuque, Iowa. The 19th. We're in full retreat. I've lost my company!"

"We're from Belvidere, near Chicago," I say. "Who told you to retreat?"

"No one. It's retreat or face certain death!"

"You can't retreat without an order," Frank says. "What's your name?"

"Piers. Piers van Kyp, sir." Piers's eyes are bluer than his jacket and they're wild in terror. "I'm lost. I'm lost."

"Piers, think carefully. Did you hear an officer order you to retreat?"

"I heard General Sturgis, sir. He said, 'If Mr. Forrest will let me alone, I will let him alone. You have done all you could. Now all you can do is to save yourselves!'"

Frank and I gape at him. "Sturgie said that?" he finally gasps.

"Yes, sir, he kept saying, 'What can we do? What can we do?'

"That's a retreat," Frank says grimly. "Back to Stubbs Farm. Run!"

Following Frank and Piers, I gather up my rifle and my kit and stagger out of the creek. Bloody water streams out of my uniform. All around us are overturned wagons and the bodies of our runaway drivers. "Stay off the Ripley–Guntown Road," Frank says. "It's the Rebs' turn to forage. Go along where the embankment meets the bottomlands. They'll be too busy climbing up to get their booty or climbing down with their hands full to reckon with us."

I go first, since Piers is from another regiment and lost. Frank takes up the rear on account of being an older man and already winded, I reckon. He falls farther and farther behind.

At dusk the Ripley–Guntown Road embankment is clogged with Rebel cookfires. The Johnnies are in high spirits, as though on a picnic supper, already drunk on the U.S. Army's coffee, hardtack, bacon, ham, cornbread, cabbages, carrots, peaches, and maple syrup. "We'd invite you to dine, Billy Yank, but then we'd have to shoot you!" a Reb crows out. His fellows laugh. One of them lets loose the Rebel yell and shoots his pistol into the air.

At twilight we pass more Rebs straining to pull our small mountain howitzers off broken-down wagons. They ignore us as they help themselves to our rifles, ammunition, and minié balls. A groaning wagonload of cannonballs overturns—every one rolls down the embankment and sinks into the bayou. The terrified team turns tail and runs down the Ripley–Guntown Road, dragging a splintering wagon behind them.

There's no one at Stubbs Farm. Piers and I sit down to wait.

It's past dark when Ira Klein and Isaac Pepper run into camp. They fall on the ground panting, holding up one index finger apiece.

I tell them, "You've got something important to say, I understand. Take your time."

"We were sent here to gather the remnants," Isaac finally says, still panting. "We've retreated to Guntown."

"On the other side of the bridge?" I ask. "Are you sayin' we're to go all the way back the way we came and then some? Isn't that where the fighting is?"

"No Johnny Rebs there now," Ira adds.

"And where are they?" I ask.

Isaac Pepper shrugs his shoulders. "All we saw were Rebs on the embankments, feasting as though they were at a Sunday-meeting potluck."

"The last Reb I saw was running into the forest with a U.S. Army ham under each arm," Ira adds.

"Did you see Frank?" I ask. They nod.

"We wait for Frank."

Frank shows his face finally. It takes another two hours to retrace our steps. Rebs have fled the embankments. Our wagons are stripped. All our war matériel has been stolen. Our horse teams have galloped off who knows where.

I'm too exhausted to care. All I can think about is curling up in my bedroll and sleeping this horrible day away.

We cross Tishomingo Creek Bridge and follow the Wire Road toward Guntown. The dim lights of a dozen campfires show us forward.

Charlie is the first to see us. "Albert! Frank! We thought the two of you were dead!"

Charlie tips his head toward the biggest campfire. We follow.

What remains of the 95th sit on sedge grass, too exhausted to even stand at attention. Their eyes blank, their jaws slack, their shoulders bowed, they lean toward Captain Almon Schellenger as a tribute to his command. The wounded lie with their heads turned toward him. There might be fifty men left.

Captain Schellenger is standing on a tree stump and yelling. Our captain grew up speaking German, in Prussia. He's so rattled his English has mostly fled.

"Men!" he yells. "How many Rebs? Don't know! How many Rebs in woods? Don't know! How many Rebs in fields? Don't know!

"Sharps & Hankins repeating carbine rifles . . . best rifles in te world. Rebs can't have tem! We have to burn—we have to burn everyting."

A great groan rises up around us. Captain Schellenger jumps off the tree stump. Gently, he places his rifle in our campfire. "I order you! Rifles, newspapers, letters from home—tey can't find anyting. Tey can't learn anyting. Quickly! Rebs are coming."

"Charlie, why is Captain Schellenger giving orders? We've never heard a peep out of him."

Charlie gasps. "Albert, you don't know! Colonel Church, Colonel Humphrey, Captain Bush, Sergeants Andrus and Euripides—they all died today. All our familiar officers led charges, and they all died today."

"Oh, no! Where's Robbie?"

"Under yon cypress, crying his eyes out."

I catch my breath. "Who else?"

"Michael McGill. Oscar Vander Zee. I haven't seen one wagon driver."

"Fall in!" Captain Schellenger yells. "Quickly! Help te lying-down ones to empty teir pockets. Afterward we scatter into te *Wald*. Te woods . . . te big woods . . . no one tere. . . ." He pounds his fists into his sides in frustration.

"Captain, the wilderness?" Frank asks. He sits down hard on the ground.

"*Ja,* into te wilderness! *Schnell! Schnell!* Quickly!"

Frank groans. "Why am I so tired?"

Captain Schellenger keeps yelling. "Burn guns, ten to Memphis!" He holds up six fingers. "West. Overland, in small groups. Trains wait tere for us. Six days to Memphis. Eighty miles maybe? Tose tat stand, help te lying-down ones to walk. Six days to Memphis. Burn guns, leave now!"

Frank hands me his rifle. "Burn mine for me, will you? I'm completely knackered."

The men pull paper bundles out of their haversacks. One by one we drop our rifles into the fire, newspaper clippings and letters from home, too. As the paper crackles, the flames shoot higher and hotter. Our newspapers and letters glow red, burn black, sink to ashes.

One by one we burn our guns in Guntown.

11

MY TRUE NAME

E HIDE OUR UNION COATS AND CAPS IN our haversacks. Frank and I have no food besides hardtack, no water, no rifles, no ammunition. Some soldiers had the presence of mind to remove the bayonets before tossing their rifles into the fire. Frank and I are completely defenseless.

"I'm sorry," I tell him. "I should have remembered the bayonets."

"That's all right. Help me up."

Piers and I help Frank to his feet. Even accounting for the June heat, Frank feels hot. I reach up and pour the last splash from my canteen onto his brow. "We'll need water right away. We'll go to the Tishomingo."

"I have to find my regiment," Piers says.

"Of course," Frank says faintly. "Good luck. Find

Robbie Horan. He always knows the way of things."
Piers runs off into the darkness.

It takes more time than I would have thought to find a curve of the Tishomingo, a black-and-silver ribbon in the starshine. Frank sits down hard again. I rush to the creek. Water glugs into our canteens. We drink them dry. I refill them. We drink them dry again.

I help Frank over the creek. He's dead weight against my shoulder. He talks incessantly. "Albert, we'll stay in the forests. See the North Star? Keep the North Star on your right shoulder to head west. Look for Venus. This time of year it's almost directly east at sunset. We'll do most of our traveling at night.

"We'll eat the tender plants around the streambeds: watercress, wild onions, and carrots. We'll forage on the small farms. . . ."

"Frank, stop! I've been a soldier as long as you have. I know what to do."

We make our way slowly through the hot, steamy night. All around us are shapes—hunched over, scuttling like crabs—the 95th on the run. We hide against a tree, then hobble to the next one, then to the next. More and more soldiers pass us. The only sounds are the dry hiss of boots on pine needles and the groans of the wounded. Soon we're bringing up the rear.

A herd of horses gallops by in an open field next to the woods. Each drags tatters of tack and harness, some Union, some Confederate. I gasp. "Frank, look!

How beautiful!" In the moonlight their hardware gleams like bits of stars fallen to earth. They are headed west, too.

I'm holding up Frank, trying to walk, trying to watch for danger.

Now there's no one in front of us.

Frank's knees buckle. He crawls toward the canopy of the nearest longleaf pine. "I have to rest. I'm sorry, Albert. Go on ahead."

I crawl in before him and lift the branches. "I'll stay with you. There'll be other trains. The 95th will be wandering into Memphis for weeks."

Frank props himself against the tree trunk with a deep moan.

"What's wrong?"

"I don't know. I'm so feverish. Every muscle and joint aches. I'm too tuckered out to walk anymore."

How long has this tree been growing here? For centuries, perhaps—it's as big around as a kitchen table. I sit next to him for an hour, maybe more. It starts to rain. The longleaf pine branches become waterlogged, heavy enough to drag on the ground. We're completely covered, dry, and sheltered.

I tuck my jacket around Frank's shoulders. As I do, the backs of my hands brush against his face. He feels on fire.

"We'll rest here till first light," I say. "You'll feel better in the morning. Here's my canteen." He takes a sip.

We're quiet, resting against the tree trunk. Just as I think he's fallen asleep, he takes a deep breath.

"What's your name?"

"You know my name. It's Albert."

Frank reaches out into the darkness, takes my far hand, and places it over his heart. "Won't you tell me your name? Please?"

I gasp. "I—I don't know what you mean." I tear my hand away.

"I thought there was something wrong with me," he says softly. "I don't remember when I figured it out. . . . The tarantula family, the black pearls, Robbie, Roland. I've never seen you shaving. I used to watch you, breathing in the scent of those Natchez magnolia blossoms."

"Please . . . please tell me your name."

"My name is Albert."

My mind races: What am I to do? I have never, never trusted anyone with my secret, not since Tom's betrayal.

"Please." He takes another deep breath. "Please," he says, fainter still.

I turn away from him. "No. You've made a mistake. My name is Albert." I say softly, "You know that's what I call myself. Albert."

Long minutes go by. The next time Frank speaks, he doesn't even try to hide the sadness in his voice. "I have a good friend in Memphis, a college friend. I spent a summer with him once, catching *Eurycea bislineata*. I can stay with him until I'm better. He's called James Everett Dennett."

"He'll be fighting with the Rebs."

"No, he won't." Frank takes another deep breath.

"We founded a club: The University of Pennsylvania's Charles Darwin Society."

"Charles who?"

"Charles Darwin. He studies animals. He's a naturalist. An Englishman. Thirty years ago he spent five years sailing around the world on a ship called the *Beagle*." Frank pauses to catch his breath. "Ever since, he's written about the animals he observed: how animals change, how they adapt, to better their lives.

"Jim and his mother will take me in. I need to sleep . . . sleep for a long time . . . the corner of North River Side Drive and Saffarans Avenue. I can walk . . . if you'll help me."

"And just leave you there? What about our hospitals in Memphis?"

"I'll be fine. I'll catch up to the 95th when I'm able."

"You'll get into trouble."

"I'll tell them I got lost. You tell them . . . I got lost."

The rain falls harder. Our refuge is so dark, I can't see one inch in front of me. "It's like we're the only people in the whole world, isn't it? Frank?"

He's finally fallen asleep.

At sunrise we wash our hardtack down with creek water. Before us is the flat land of northwestern Mississippi, floodplain of the Mississippi River, as flat as northwestern Illinois. It feels like home.

Dark pine trees smudge the horizon in every direction. There is no one in the fields or on the muddy track roads. There is no one to stop us. We don't have to hide from anyone. Yet it takes all morning to walk about three miles.

Frank takes another deep breath. "I have to rest again."

We sit under another longleaf pine.

"How old are you?"

I'm so surprised that I stammer out the truth. "I—I don't know. I was old enough to remember my mother dying. I was four, maybe five. Two years in New York, two years in Illinois, two years in the army. It's in Ireland that the years are muddled. My guess? I'm seventeen."

"I'm twenty-one."

I grin at him. "You're an old man, Frank Moore."

His green-blue eyes shine. "I'm old enough to know what I want."

He closes his eyes. Just as I think he's fallen asleep, he takes another deep breath. His eyes are open, vacant. He's radiating heat. For the first time I begin to worry: What's wrong with him?

"Would you . . . could you go back to skirts again?"

"My name is Albert," I say flatly. "Your fever has gone to your head."

"I don't want you to be anything you're not at this very moment. But our lives would be easier with you in skirts. We could go away after the war. San Francisco. London. Dublin. Australia. Some-place no one knows you."

"London?" Another sort of life blooms in front of me for an instant.

"'If you're tired of London, you're tired of life.' Or so they say."

"Let's get you to Memphis. Sleep."

"I've been dreaming about you. We're free. We're laughing."

"Your fever has gone to your head, Frank. Go to sleep."

I fall asleep with my head against his shoulder. I dream about the two of us in a forest I don't recognize. No war, no people—just us, happy.

At twilight he wakes up again.

Frank takes a long pull from his canteen. "Tell me about yourself," I say. "It's your turn. Eat this hardtack first."

He breaks the hardtack in half and gives one piece to me.

"I grew up in Providence, Rhode Island. My grandfather was a blacksmith. My father is a blacksmith. I went to college at sixteen. My parents are so proud: a college-educated Moore, the first in the family. I saw an advertisement in one of the Chicago newspapers for a schoolteacher and came west."

He takes another deep breath. "You asked about Charles Darwin. His work is all about change. Most times, change is so slow we can't see it, even though it's happening right before our eyes. Change is progress. Hard, but progress."

He falls silent. Just when I think he's asleep, he murmurs, "Don't change."

I say with a smile, "I thought you said change is progress."

"Don't change."

"Put your head on my shoulder. I promise not to change." We both smell like the Tishomingo, and gunpowder, blood, and sweat.

"Do you know that song Robbie Horan is always singing? 'The Harp of Green Erin and the Banner of Stars'?"

"I know some of the verses, bits and pieces mostly."

"I'd like to hear what you remember."

I sing softly, as though a lullaby:

"The war trumpet has sounded, our rights
    are in danger;
Shall the brave sons of Erin be deaf to the
    call?
When freedom demands of both native
    and stranger,
Her aid, lest the greatest of nations
    should fall? . . .

"I swear by the love that we bear our old
    Sire-land,
And the vows we have pledged to the home
    of the free,
As we'd sheathed our swords in the foes of
    dear Ireland,
We will use them as freely 'gainst traitors
    to thee. . . .

"Oh, long may our flags wave in union
   together,
And the Harp of Green Erin still kiss the
   same breeze,
And brave ev'ry storm that beclouds the
   fair weather,
Till our Harp, like the Stars, floats o'er
   rivers and seas. . . ."

We walk on. We eat wild onions and carrots. We forage in abandoned, blighted farms for anything to eat. Always, Frank's arm is draped across my shoulder; we are as close as two people can be.

We stop to rest every couple of miles. Under the deep shade of a tupelo, Frank falls silent. As his feet and hands start to twitch, I know he's under the deepest layers of sleep. He's dreaming of marching and shooting.

"All right," I say softly. "I'll give you what you want, Francis Patrick Moore. My name is Jennie Margaret Hodgers. I wore trousers to work as a shepherd for the bishop of Belfast. I was Georgie Hodgers in Queens. Tom couldn't abide me doing better than he in America. He betrayed me at the O'Banions' All Souls' Day dinner. I had to leave the good job the bishop got for me. Then I worked as a farmhand for Mr. Cleary. It was his brother who got me that good job.

"You don't understand about that, being American born. We Irish have to stand together, for no one will stand for us.

"It feels as though I've been running, Frank, running my whole life." Tears slide down my face. No one's here to see them, so I let them slide.

"In Belvidere I sometimes thought about borrowing one of Fiona Cleary's dresses. Just bite the bullet; just get it over with—show the world I'm Jennie Hodgers. But had I showed myself—what then? Mr. Cleary couldn't have kept me on. Women don't bust sod or break the new ground. I'd have had to work as a Belvidere housemaid. Sure, wouldn't I be a terrible housemaid? Aside from my rifle, I've never cleaned anything in my life."

I wipe my face with my U.S. Army washcloth. "It was easier to lie. But the truth has come out twice now—with the O'Banions and now with you. So I run. I'm free and trapped, male and female, and all at the same time.

"I trust you, Frank Moore, but I've seen men with their sweethearts. A soldier's life is hard: Time and again you've tried to make mine easier. So my secret would come out all the same, and I'd have to run from you. I have to keep my secret to stay close to you.

"I used to tell myself: We are who we say we are. That isn't true, for we don't know where to stop, do we? How do we know what's been invented out of whole cloth and what is really, truly us? As our true selves we are set apart from one another, true enough, but to live a lie sets us apart further still, as a narrow river valley widens as the stream gains speed to the sea."

Frank sleeps till sunset, then wakes. We walk until dawn.

On a farmer's tree line I find a magnolia with a few blossoms left. I take them back to our hideout under a tupelo tree. "Frank, look, magnolia blossoms!" But Frank is already asleep. I scatter them around us, and dream of butter cookies and tart lemonade.

It takes us more than three weeks to reach Memphis. The Union stronghold is crowded with soldiers, hundreds of them. They tread the sidewalks with sure confidence. They don't even break their strides, laughing and shouting to one another, as civilians step into the muddy streets to avoid them. No one gives us more than a glance.

The corner of North River Side Drive and Saffarans looks untouched by the war. Birds chirp in the pear and apple trees in the side lawns. Sturdy houses of whitewashed brick stand back from the quiet street. Flowers I've never seen before bloom in sunny gardens. It's as though this patch of Memphis and its inhabitants are doing everything they can to ignore the troop boats and gunboats docked a stone's throw away in the Mississippi.

We stand in front of the Dennetts' front door for a moment. Frank is a bag of bones, leaning against me. He sways upright on his own two feet.

"When I'm able, I'll go to Memphis headquarters and join the 95th again. I'll tell them I was living off the land—foraging. I wish you'd tell me your name," he says softly, "for you're the bravest person I've ever met."

"I'm no braver than you, or anyone else in the 95th."

Frank squares his shoulders, then raps sharply with the door knocker. An older woman opens the door. At the sight of our Union blue, I reckon, her face turns chalk white in cold hatred.

"Mrs. Dennett? Do you remember me? I'm Frank Moore."

Her face changes immediately. "Mr. Moore!" Quickly she pulls us into the hall and shuts the door. "James is in his study. He'll be so happy to see you. James!" she calls down the hall. "You'll never guess who's here! It's Frank!"

James Everett Dennett is in a sunny room off the parlor. All around him are stuffed animals, reptiles, and birds. On every surface are stacks of open books. Behind him are more books, crammed into shelves from floor to ceiling. He reels his wheelchair back, open-mouthed in terror, at the sight of me in my uniform. Afraid of me!

"Jim, it's good to see you! Private Albert Cashier's a good friend. He won't hurt you."

"Frank, you look terrible," James says cheerfully.

"You look considerably worse. You've lost another foot since college."

James chuckles. "My doctor says no sugar, which is easy as pie, what with the war on."

"Have you a doctor? I've got pneumonia, or

maybe just influenza. Malaria? Something. I'm so tired all the time."

I help Frank to a sofa. He collapses onto it with a groan. I long to put a pillow under his head, but I resist making a gesture that might seem feminine. Mrs. Dennett says, "I'll fetch a blanket."

"We've come from Guntown, Mississippi," I tell James. "We've had to cross overland to our rallying point here in Memphis. Frank hopes to stay here until he's better."

"Of course he can stay here. He mustn't go to the army hospitals. They're death traps."

"Albert? We don't know yet why people who are sick together get sicker, why they share one another's diseases. They weaken and become sicker still. Someday we'll know. Meanwhile, Jim's right. If you're sick or wounded, stay out of the hospitals if you can. Find the 95th."

Frank sticks his hand out for me to shake. It feels as hot and loose as a turkey drumstick still on the bird, fresh out of the oven.

"Take care," I say softly. I look at James in his wheelchair.

James puts his hands up. "What I have can't be caught. He's safe here. Frank, you can stay in the back bedroom, just like last time."

Frank locks his gaze into mine. There's a bit of the old twinkle in his eyes. "You must be feeling better. Your voice doesn't sound like you're sick anymore."

I grin back. "It comes and goes."

154

"Private Cashier—I will see you when I return to the 95th."

"Yes, Private Moore. I will see you soon. What did you say you were catching that summer when you were here? It sounded like our sergeant's name. Sergeant Euripides?" I let go of his hand.

Frank closes his eyes. It's as though he's saved all his strength for this moment, and now that strength is gone. Mrs. Dennett tenderly tucks a blanket around him. I hand her a sofa pillow. "Aren't you sweet!" she exclaims. "I'll take good care of Frank. He needs broth for strength and medicinal tea for his fever."

Gently, she cradles his head and places the pillow under it.

"I reckon I should go."

James says, "We were catching *Eurycea bislineata*. Is that what he said? The two-lined salamander—it lives in seepages, in floodplains, and in creek beds. It has two distinct lines along its sides from head to tail."

James rolls over to a cupboard and lifts a stuffed salamander out of it.

"This is a good specimen. Frank caught this one. We wanted to catch them because of their twin lines but also because of their flat tails. We wondered why their tails are flat. It's a rarity among the salamander species. They live only in the lower Mississippi floodplain."

"Frank said the two of you founded a society. Charles somebody?"

James laughs. "The University of Pennsylvania's Charles Darwin Society. Darwin spent five years at sea and kept a meticulous journal. He's written about his voyage for years now. He's gotten himself into trouble with his latest book, *On the Origin of Species*. I ordered it from a New York bookseller before the war."

Mrs. Dennett tosses her head. "What nonsense! Men from monkeys!"

"Charles Darwin thinks we're monkeys?" I ask in amazement.

"He didn't write that, but it is a logical progression," James says. "His book is pure scientific inquiry. Why do we share the same skeletal and muscular structure? Why do both monkeys and men prefer to live in groups? The highest order of monkeys—they're the primates—is the only animal with no tail. Just like us, Mother."

As I'm nodding politely it occurs to me—James sounds just like Frank.

Mrs. Dennett tucks another blanket around Frank's feet as he snores softly. "I'll make him some willow tea," she whispers.

Mrs. Dennett reminds me of the ladies of Natchez. She's so kind. What a blessing it must be: to be so kind to everyone.

12

THE CAPE DE VERDE OCTOPUS

---

*F*ROM MEMPHIS THE 95TH IS SENT UPRIV-
er to St. Louis to guard prisoners. We load them
onto steamboats and send them up the Mississippi
River; then they go up the Illinois River and are
marched overland to Camp Douglas on Chicago's
South Side. It feels strange to know that these men
will see home long before I do. They'll feel the
Great Lakes autumn and winter while I'm still in
the war.

On Tuesday, November 8, we vote in the field,
and of course I vote for President Lincoln. He's
brought us through a long and terrible fight. He deserves another four years, a peacetime presidency
this time.

Afterward it occurs to me that I might have been
the only female in America to vote. I'm not even old

enough to vote yet, much less a man. Charlie's not old enough to vote either, but he said if anyone deserves to cast a ballot, it's us. I have to agree with him.

As General Canby passed out ballots, he didn't ask any of us if we were old enough. The general must think we deserve to vote as well.

In March the 95th is sent south and stationed on Dauphin Island off the coast of Mobile, Alabama. We merged with the 2nd Brigade of the 16th Army Corps. General Edward Canby's directive is to lay siege to two Confederate forts on Dauphin: Fort Blakely and Fort Spanish.

We are siege experts now. But the sandy soil here can't be molded into trenches. It won't stay put—it's like playing sand castles. We have to fight in the dunes, flat on our stomachs.

We fight our way, inch by inch, one division toward Fort Blakely, the other toward Fort Spanish. For both armies, though, the fighting is subdued, almost halfhearted. I think the Rebs know they're going to lose this war. We certainly know we're going to win.

We fight by day and throw hand grenades by night.

On April 8 the Rebs surrender all of Dauphin Island. The 95th is one the first regiments to march into Fort Spanish.

Immediately, the forts become a holding pen for more prisoners. Either we're catching them or they're surrendering, by the thousands now. They seem grateful to be caught: They grudgingly give up their guns, but then they want to know what's for supper and could they send letters home?

The Rebs know they can't win—why be the last man to die for a certain defeat? So they surrender in waves. The Union know we will win—why die now, just weeks—maybe days—from certain victory? So we don't take chances, either.

Dauphin Island is beautiful, ringed with sand dunes. The sand is perfect for our tents after camping in mud for more than two years. There are oyster-shell piles, twenty feet high in places. Some in the 95th think these piles were left here by the Spanish and French. I think they're older than that. Native people must have been throwing oyster shells onto these piles for centuries. We climb the piles just for fun.

General Canby says the Spanish and French colonists planted the palm trees along the shoreline. Scrub pines, palmettos, and live oaks grow in the salt marshes. The swamps are jumping with mullet.

Charlie Ives has learned to climb the palm trees barefoot. He knocks the coconuts out with his new rifle. We drink the coconut milk, roast mullet filets and coconut flesh over a campfire, and pretend we're pirates.

It's hot again, but there's always a Gulf breeze. When I'm not on guard duty, I roll up my pants and wade barefoot in the warm water. The waves pound the shore, then grate against it, endlessly, endlessly. I hadn't realized how much I missed the ocean.

As the moon waxes, bigger and brighter in the night sky, the sand dunes boil up with baby sea turtles, of all things. By the hundreds they waddle frantically toward the Gulf as the moon sheds its silvery light. I've never seen turtles move so fast. They don't waddle the beach during the day. I wonder why not. The moon sheds light, true enough, but not as much as the sun.

If they use the moon to guide them, how can they know it's a full moon up there when they're hidden in the sand down here?

In the morning pelicans and cormorants skim the surface of the water. They dive headfirst into the shallows and come up with food in their beaks. Just as the offshore breeze cools the afternoon, we toss hardtack to a school of porpoises. Somehow they know when the day begins to cool. They've learned to come back for food at that same moment day after day.

Where is Frank?

It's been almost a year, July through April, without a word. I don't dare write to the Dennetts for fear of putting them or Frank in danger. He has to know where we're stationed. Memphis headquarters must know where we are.

Maybe he's still sick? Maybe he's decided he's had enough of war? Frank doesn't strike me as a deserter. He believes in the Union as much as any of us. How are we to find each other? He knows I can't go back to Belvidere.

San Francisco. London. Dublin. Australia. Even

Texas would make a fine fresh start. In my mind's eye I see myself putting that sofa pillow under Frank's head. I've almost convinced myself that I did it, and not Mrs. Dennett. It was my idea; no one could dispute it.

Aren't you sweet! Surely Frank heard Mrs. Dennett say that. Surely he knew she was referring to me. Were his eyes already closed? I don't remember. Maybe he thought it was I who cradled his head so gently, nesting the pillow under him.

Frank said Charles Darwin's work is all about change.

The sunset off Dauphin Island stretches out to encompass the entire western edge of the horizon. As far as the eye can see, the Gulf of Mexico is lit up in brilliant reds and oranges. Thinking about change has made my mind do the same thing. It's been stretched out, lit up more than I ever thought possible.

San Francisco. London. Dublin. Australia. The whole world is waiting for us, stretching out her arms in welcome.

Aren't you sweet! Yes, yes I am, and don't you forget it, Frank Moore.

The days roll by. We hear a rumor one morning that the war has ended in Appomattox, Virginia, one week gone already. General Robert E. Lee has surrendered to our own Major General Ulysses S. Grant. General Canby tells us to stay in ranks until he receives confirmation by wire.

I guard prisoners as they wait in line to eat. I

never did get to ask Frank about why these poor men of the South are fighting for—no, fought for—the rich slaveholders. I can tell by their accents and temperaments that these prisoners are mountain men, and hardscrabble farmers. None of them would feel at home in those grand plantations on the Indianola Road.

These men are Scots-Irish, the fiery Ulstermen who were our neighbors back in Belfast—neighbors, but not friends.

I ask a group of prisoners, "If you warn't slavers, why'd you fight us, then?"

They stand thoughtful for a moment, holding tin plates at the ready.

"Because you're here," their leader says, finally.

They look as though they have nothing left worth fighting for. Change will fall hard upon them, for the Union will not so easily forgive and forget.

I guard them again as they board prison ships for Camp Douglas. "Good luck to you," I say. Some of them look upon me angrily. Most look half surprised, half relieved, that I am are wishing them well.

When I see you again, Frank Moore, I'll tell you my one true name.

"Albert?" Charlie interrupts my thoughts. "You sure do like to wade in the Gulf of Mexico."

"It reminds me of Ireland," I tell him. "I used to wade in the North Channel off the Island Magee. But this water is like bathwater. The North Channel used to turn my toes blue, it was so cold."

162

"You have a package. Colonel Blanton has it in the officers' tent. "

Colonel Blanton glares at me from his desk. "Private Cashier, would you care to tell me why you have a package sent all the way from Memphis headquarters? I understand you have never received any mail from anyone."

Colonel Blanton is nothing like Colonel Humphrey or Colonel Church. He's distrustful of the men, and for no reason. Hence we don't trust him. If he's so sure we're hiding something, what's *he* hiding?

"I don't know, Colonel Blanton. It could be anything."

The colonel is holding the package. My package.

I wait patiently. It's from Frank! It's word from Frank! The Dennetts did the clever thing, somehow getting Memphis headquarters to mail it. A private address in Memphis would have aroused all sorts of suspicion.

Colonel Blanton waits, but I can wait him out. I wait. And wait. It's against the law to open a soldier's mail. He knows that.

"Here."

I snatch the package away and run for my tent.

It could be anything! Anything! With a pounding heart I tear open the wrapping paper. Inside is a book: *The Voyage of the Beagle* by Charles Darwin. There's a letter in the middle. I don't recognize the handwriting; the letter is not from Frank. Disappointment covers me like a blanket.

Dear Private Cashier,

Our mutual friend, Frank Moore, assured me that you could read this book and understand it. He was most insistent that I send it to you. He asked that you pay particular attention to the opening pages about the Cape de Verde octopus, off the coast of Africa.

I am taking the liberty of writing down the lines he wanted you to see.

In the words of Charles Darwin:

"I was much interested, on several occasions, by watching the habits of an octopus, or cuttle-fish. Although common in the pools of water left by the retiring tide, these animals were not easily caught. By means of their long arms and suckers, they could drag their bodies into very narrow crevices; and when thus fixed, it required great force to remove them. . . . These animals also escaped detection by a very extraordinary, chameleon-like power of changing their color. They appear to vary their tints according to the nature of the ground over which they pass: when in deep water, their general shade was brownish purple, but when placed on the land, or in shallow water, this dark tint changed into one of a yellowish green. . . . These changes were effected in such a manner, that clouds, varying in tint between hyacinth red and chestnut brown, were continually passing over the body."

I flip the letter over impatiently, then flip it back again. Why on earth does Frank want to tell me about an octopus? "The Irish!" I mutter angrily. "They will tell their stories! Frank! Where are you?"

> *The Cape de Verde octopus can change its colors to protect itself and thus live a better life. It's called adaptation. Frank asked me to tell you that he understood why you had to change your colors. You wanted a better life too.*
>
> *Private Cashier, it is so difficult to tell you this, forgive me for not writing to you sooner. Frank died just two weeks after you left him in our care. We couldn't send him home to Rhode Island, and my mother was afraid to alert the Grand Army of the Republic's Occupational Forces here in Memphis. We buried him in our family plot in the churchyard of the First Episcopal Church of Memphis. A neighbor will take this parcel to your headquarters, once we've saved up enough money for the postage.*
>
> *I wish to extend to you all my sympathy. Frank was a good friend and a humble, patient naturalist. Please visit us after the war. You will be extended all courtesies, as befitting a friend of Frank Moore.*
>
> *Both Frank and I agreed that Charles Darwin could not approve of this War Between the States, although to our knowledge he hasn't said a word about it. It has been such a waste. All these good men have died for what would have happened*

*anyway. That is, the liberation of our slaves. I'm
sure Charles Darwin would agree with me when I
say that no civilization has ever progressed with
a good number of its people enslaved. Darwin
would say that the human race lives best in
groups as long as we are each free to pursue our
better lives.*

Sincerely,
James Everett Dennett

It's another waxing moon, and I walk into the
Gulf with every intention of not stopping. Just keep
walking. Just get it over with. How many decades
will I have to live without Frank? Four, five maybe?
Fifty years! Fifty years of knowing I didn't trust
him enough to give him my one true name when I
had the chance. Even worse, he died knowing I
didn't trust him enough.

This is my penance, I think in horror. *Fifty years!
Because I didn't trust him enough to make amends.*

I'm free and trapped, and I don't have the
strength to run as a solitary any longer.

Small creatures bobble against the small of my
back, my elbows. It's more baby sea turtles, paddling
frantically out to sea. Why do they come out at
night?

Tears come, because all of a sudden I can hear
Frank telling me in his bright and eager voice: Baby
sea turtles know enough to come out at night, in
order to hide from the hungry pelicans and cormorants that hunt by day.

With my bayonet I slice open my wartime constant companion. My heaving sobs come out at
night to hide too, as my tears fall and are lost forever in the salt sea.

13

MUSTERED OUT

August 18, 1865
United States Registered Mail

The Dennetts
North River Side Drive and Saffarans Avenue
Memphis, Tennessee, U.S.A.

Dear James Dennett,
    Please don't be alarmed about the U.S. regis-
tered mail. I use it as a precaution only.
    Although the war has been over for months
now, the 95th was mustered out just yesterday.
    With this letter I am sending you and your
mother two strands of black pearls Frank gave to
me. Although I read Charles Darwin's book and
he said nothing about them, I sure he would ap-

*prove of black pearls. The oysters that make them
must be darker than regular oysters. White pearls
would stand out too much, and it would be too
easy for the pearl fishers to take them. The dark
oysters didn't change their colors. They changed
the color of their pearls instead.*

*I like Charles Darwin's book. I reckon I un-
derstand what he means, that animals adapt over
time, generations of gradual change. I don't believe animals decide to adapt, though.*

*People decide to adapt. They can change
overnight if they really set their minds to it.*

*I'm also enclosing fifty-two United States dol-
lars.*

*Maybe I'll visit you someday. Thank you for
telling me about Frank. He was a good friend. He
made this unbearable war bearable.*

> *Sincerely,*
> *Albert Cashier*
> *Aboard the* Molly Able
> *en route to St. Louis*

I look over Robbie's shoulder as he writes. "What
a good fist you've got, Robbie. I can see why the officers wanted you to write the meeting notes and
dispatches. My writing looks like turkey scratch."

Robbie says nothing, bent over his work. Finally,
he sits up and shakes his right hand about to loosen
the muscles. "For you, no charge," he says with a grin.
"Fifty-two dollars is a lot of money. Four months'
pay."

169

"They need it and I can spare it. They did a better job taking care of Frank than we ever could."

"He gave you pearls?" he asks softly. "He stayed in a Reb household?"

"James was his chum from college," I say coldly. "Remember foraging the plantations on the Indianola Road? What have you got in *your* pockets, Robbie?"

He turns red. "I'm going home to Belvidere. Are you?"

"No. Isaac Pepper is going to Saunemin. He's inherited some land there. He wants to start a tree nursery business and wants me for a partner."

"Where's Saunemin?"

"He says it's between Pontiac and Kankakee in Livingston County, Illinois."

"Oh. Downstate, then. Not a lot of Irish downstate. Well, good luck." Robbie tries a broader smile.

"Goodbye," I say, colder still. I pick up my letter and turn away.

Because of you, Robbie, Frank spent his last Christmas in the brig! We didn't speak for months because of you, and now he's gone forever. I'll never forgive you.

In St. Louis I give myself two months of doing nothing but indulging my idleness, as a present to myself. I have never had this much leisure time in my life. I sleep late and take my time over breakfast, sipping coffee. I walk along the Mississippi and Missouri riverbanks. I read books and newspapers. I take long naps in the middle of the day. I watch the sun tilt toward Australia, as the leaves in the cottonwood trees turn autumnal.

I'm invited again and again into the houses of townspeople for suppers and dinners. If I eat and drink in a tavern, the owner waves away my money. I chop wood for my landlady—a Union war widow—in lieu of rent. Her young sons want to hear my war stories again and again. I don't disappoint them.

By the middle of October I'm ready to work again, but first I want to pick up my bounty. It would never do to have the Clearys know I was in Belvidere. Even worse: that I was in town and didn't come out to the farm to visit them. I decide to draw my sixty dollars in Chicago.

The main office of the First Bank of Chicago is a grand affair: high copper ceilings, marble floors, carpets, Boston ferns, and statuary. Gilt-framed portraits of stern, prosperous-looking bankers glare at us from the walls.

A bank secretary approaches me. "May I help you, sir?"

"My name is Albert Cashier. The First Bank of Chicago, Belvidere Branch, has been holding a bounty for the soldiers of Boone County since August 1862. The 95th Illinois, Infantry; I've come to collect my bounty."

"Of course. The bank president, Mr. Talbot, likes to meet returning soldiers when they come in. I'll tell him you're here, Mr. Cashier."

In no time at all an older man comes out of an office, hand outstretched. It's been so long since I've seen expensive, tailored clothes. I drink in his banker's gray three-piece suit. His black shoes are mirror bright. I can't wait to get out of my threadbare Union blue and into fine clothes again.

He's sporting dundrearies—long, wide sideburns to the chin but with no beard.

"I'm sorry to say you'll have to wait, Mr. Cashier," he says smoothly. "It's going to take a few days for Belvidere to telegraph a bank draft."

"I don't mind. I'll stay in a boarding house or something. I've become addicted to reading the newspapers."

"Splendid." Mr. Talbot looks me over. "Tell me, are you looking for work?"

I stand up straight. "I'm always looking for work."

"You could help close Camp Douglas while you wait. The city of Chicago wants to close the camp quickly and is paying top dollar. The people here would like to put the prisoner-of-war camp behind us. I'm sure you understand."

"There aren't any prisoners left, then?"

"Oh, no. The last of them signed the loyalty oath to the United States and were sent home in August. The camp was not far from here, on the corner of Cottage Grove and Thirty-fifth Street. Out the front door, turn left. You can't miss it."

The bank president beams at me, surely an overbright smile for a man in his position. "It used to be

172

Senator Stephen Douglas's estate: Okenwald. Okenwald was just lovely. The rhododendrons were such a joy every May. It was the pride of Chicago's South Side. We'd like to restore it. Quickly."

"I'll look into it."

"Splendid. I'll just need to see your mustering-out papers as identification. I'll wire the Belvidere branch personally."

On the corner of Cottage Grove and 35th Street, men in tattered Union blue step out of a trench, pulling a sledge full of dirt behind them. They lift the sledge and tip it into a deep-sided wagon. Another veteran drives the wagon down Cottage Grove Avenue.

It's the end of October. Already snowflakes blow sideways, caught in a brisk wind off Lake Michigan. How I remember these long, cold winters!

I find the foreman. "Mr. Talbot from the First Bank of Chicago sent me."

The foreman is handing out shovels to more veterans. "Two dollars a day for as long as the work lasts," he barks in my direction.

"The digging is confined to that trench." He points to a trench about forty feet wide, maybe three hundred feet long, near the street. He glares at me. "Do you want to work or not?"

How hard can shoveling dirt be? And the ground is so soft already. The sod has been busted long since. The foreman reminds me of Sergeant Andrus. I'll just follow orders; I'm sure to hear the why of it sometime today.

173

I grab a shovel, sign onto the payroll, slide down the trench, and commence to dig.

Bones.

I reel back in shock. I'm knee deep in bones.

Human bones.

"The prisoners," I exclaim. "The skeletons of the prisoners!"

Despite the cold, the man next to me wipes his forehead with a handkerchief. I'd recognize that scrap of cloth anywhere. It's a Union washcloth, well used and threadbare.

"Aye, it's a bit of a jolt at first, lad. But you get used to it. I've been here from the start. We've been going at it for a month now."

"You're Irish?"

He grins at me. "So are you. Name's O'Neill. Patrick. County Limerick."

"Name's Cashier. Albert. Belfast."

"The foreman said more than twenty-six thousand prisoners were sent to Camp Douglas. Only two thousand were sent home in August. So where were you, Albert?"

I have come to realize this means where did I fight in the war.

"Mississippi, Alabama, and Louisiana. Vicksburg. Natchez. The Tombigbee River. Guntown. Dauphin Island. St. Louis."

"You were in Vicksburg? So was I. Wasn't that the grandest Fourth of July you'd ever seen? You know about the heat, then. Most of these Rebs had never seen frost before. It was the Chicago winters that killed them. That and the smallpox and dysentery."

O'Neill shovels up a pile of crisscrossed rib, arm, and jaw bones. He drops them onto a waiting sledge, where they clatter against more bones. Another man with a much bigger shovel than mine tosses four skulls into the sledge. They knock together like cannonballs.

In the freshening wind, tattered shreds of gray Confederate cloth shudder against bones. As it snows harder, it's impossible to see where the tangle of gray cloth, gray bones, and gray snow begins and ends.

There are no blankets, no trousers, shirts, socks, or gloves, not so much as an old boot in the trench. The living stripped the dead of everything they could use, in the hopes that they wouldn't end up in the trench as well.

"Thanks be to God for the snow, Albert. Before the cold weather came, we were breathing in their dust."

"I guarded these prisoners, Patrick," I tell him. "These were the very men we sent upriver from Vicksburg, from St. Louis, from Dauphin Island. We thought they were so lucky. They were going to see home before we did."

Patrick O'Neill grunts. "Their prison camps were far worse than ours. If their army was always hungry, how much food do you think they gave our boys? Serves them right, if you ask me."

"No one deserves this. We'll be sending these bones south, then?"

Patrick O'Neill stops digging long enough to

laugh. "When pigs fly! Chicago's a rough town, lad. Always has been. These wagonloads are going to a deeper trench in Oak Woods Cemetery. These Rebs will be buried"—he chuckles—"in hasty reverence. Chicago is in no mood to be generous, not after one of theirs shot President Lincoln. Those that are intact will get coffins. Those that aren't will get another trench. That's all."

Patrick and I pull the sledge full of bones up to the surface.

On the other side of Cottage Grove Avenue are expansive homes with wide porticoes and carriage houses, rolling lawns, shade trees, orchards, and rose gardens. The gentry lived just across the street from Camp Douglas. These dying men could look over this fence and see Chicagoans of quality walking their dogs, gardening, taking their carriages out for Sunday drives. Christmas parties. Easter egg hunts. May baskets. Fourth of July picnics.

This must be where that bank president, Mr. Talbot, lives! No wonder he sent me to work here.

"So much hatred! On both sides!" I exclaim. "How will we ever be a nation again?"

Patrick O'Neill looks at me sharply. "You're looking for work, aren't you, lad? Once the ground freezes, the work will shut down till spring."

I drop my shovel on the ground. "I'm not looking for this. Thousands of skeletons! Thousands! The very men I sent here! I never want to look on the face of war again."

14

February 1911

FOR ALMOST FIFTY YEARS IT HAS BEEN MY contention that a house isn't a home without good locks, a good many good locks.

My employer from years ago, the farmer Joshua Cheseboro, built my one-room house on a bit of land he owns in town. I have a bed, a rug, a sink and draining board, a cupboard, a bureau, a table, a rocking chair, a Franklin stove, and a window.

I'm quite proud of my garden out back. My cabbages are huge. My onions are the size of softballs. My potatoes have never had a touch of the blight. My three Boston Belle apple trees are beautiful in the spring, covered with blossoms in the softest pink. What is so rare as a day in June? I stand among them in wonder, breathing in their delicate scent. I look forward to their beauty all year.

Not that I've ever said as much to anyone. That would strike these small-town folk as a feminine remark, and tongues would wag. Mississippi's magnolias gave me a keen appreciation for flowers. The big, tall flowers—the hollyhocks and lupines—are in the front yard for all the world to see. The delicate tiny ones—lilies of the valley, violets, and impatiens—are hidden in the backyard.

Much of my life has remained so private as to be buried alive.

I get my constant companions from the Sears catalogue, sent to A. Cashier. I have learned to eat sparingly, mostly vegetables, or the constant companions will do me no good.

My house has just the one door. I have six locks—dead bolts, padlocks, chains—and I've saved up for a seventh.

I'm obliged to keep my window unlocked and open on summer nights. On a hot twilight years ago—it was in early September—I saw three boys in my backyard, as bold as brass, eating my Boston Belle apples. To protect my secret I sit up on hot nights, dozing with my Colonel Samuel Colt pistol on my lap.

Lately, my mind hasn't been as sharp as it used to be. What if I make a mistake and mark myself as female? There have been times when I've forgotten my pretense entirely. It's better to have a good many locks.

I nod to my neighbors. Occasionally they nod back.

I have marched, in full uniform, as a member of the Grand Army of the Republic in every Decoration Day parade for more than forty years. My second Sharps & Hankins carbine rifle, the one I received after Guntown, is just for show now, having rusted solid back in 1888.

My neighbor, Mrs. Mary Lannon, has sewn and resewn the worn seams in my uniform again and again. I've enjoyed Saturday supper with the Lannons for decades. Mrs. Lannon has always been so kind to me.

Generations of Saunemin boys have taken to calling me Drummer Boy. Like clockwork, the older boys teach the younger ones.

Every year there are fewer and fewer of us Civil War veterans in the parade. Time passes, and people either forget or don't know any better in the first place. But not us. Veterans are old men who can never forget the boys we left on the battlefield. Why did we live? Why did they die? No one knows. What we can do is remember them.

Muttonchops, burnsides, dundrearies, and handlebar mustaches are the fashion, as are full beards. It's my smooth face on parade the boys of Saunemin jeer at, even though I have a shaving mug, shaving soap, straight razor, and shaving brush prominently displayed on my sink's draining board.

I have invited every boy in Saunemin (and their sisters, too) into my home for cookies and tea. In the summer months we have our cookies and tea in the front yard, among the big, tall flowers. After we're finished, I ask them to take their plates and glasses to the sink.

In this manner, and in all seasons, they have each seen my porcelain shaving mug and matching brush, boy after boy, decade after decade. I'm careful to use the shaving soap to wash with, for everyone knows shaving soap smells like either lemon verbena or bayberry.

Our state senator, Senator Ira Lish, uses Windsor brand bayberry shaving soap. I prefer Windsor brand bayberry shaving soap, too.

I've been working odd jobs for Senator Lish for the past ten years.

When it's time to buy shaving soap, I always ask Mr. Linden, of Mr. Linden's General Store, for it in a good, loud voice. The best time to ask is on a Saturday morning. That's when the boys are out of school and skulking around the store, indulging their idleness.

"Another cake of Windsor brand bayberry shaving soap, Mr. Linden. Senator Lish and I are partial to the same brand and same scent."

"Yes, sir, Mr. Cashier. I've a good price on suspenders today."

"My suspenders are fine, Mr. Linden, but I do thank you for asking. I need a new pair of galoshes, though. I'll be shoveling snow for Senator and Mrs. Lish this afternoon."

"Yes, sir."

The boys stand in front of the Franklin stove. I

regard them as they regard me. I know they heard me speak up about shaving soap, suspenders, galoshes, and shoveling snow. I know I comport myself as a man on these Saturday mornings. There should never be any question about that.

I have never been afraid of work. Since the war I've worked as a nurseryman, a shepherd, a haymaker, a thresher man, a teamster, a lamplighter, a janitor, a snow plowman, and a general handyman. My war pension started in 1907, when I was too old to work my twelve hours a day. For the first time since I was mustered out in St. Louis, I have the luxury of leisure time.

I still like to work, though. It keeps me busy.

On Decoration Day I'm one of many. When I take my purchases out onto the street, I'm alone. I brace myself for their jeers. When they come, I'm ready.

The boys circle me like a wolf pack around a lamb. "Drummer Boy! Drummer Boy!"

"I was a fighting infantryman!" I shout. "I fought at the Siege of Vicksburg!" I flail at them with my walking stick. They just laugh.

"Crazy old man!" the bravest of them shouts. One of their dogs sinks his teeth into my pants cuff.

"I'll poison your dog! Don't think I won't poison your dog!"

"Buster! C'mere, Buster!"

Buster's eyes brighten. Even with my cuff well within his jaws, he bares his teeth at me. I slap his flank with my walking stick. To my great satisfaction, Buster looks stunned and amazed, offended, even. His mouth drops open.

A boy comes out of nowhere and scoops up Buster. The boy looks to be about eleven, maybe twelve years old. Today's generation is so tall! He's much taller than I am.

"You poison my dog and you'll be sorry."

"Don't you make me poison your dog!"

"You'll get a rock through your window, Drummer Boy!"

"And you'll get a dead dog! I know where you live. You're Steven Altschuler and I know where you live. You think Mr. Linden doesn't sell rat poison? I've bought rat poison from him a dozen times."

"Let's go," another boy shouts. "He's just a crazy old man. Everyone in town knows he's just a crazy old Irishman."

"I was a fighting infantryman! I've worked hard all my life. I've been in America since before your parents were born!"

"See ya next time, Drummer Boy."

"Drummer Boy! Drummer Boy! Crazy Irish Drummer Boy!"

The boys skim the fence with the effortlessness of youth. Steven has Buster over one shoulder. As Buster skims the fence, he gets in one last growl. I growl back.

Home. I unlock, rush inside, and lock up again, six times, plus the chain. I stack firewood to the doorknob: no boys, no Buster. I'm free.

I will go to Mr. Linden's General Store tomorrow

for that seventh lock. It's a York lock, with both a combination and a key. I've been admiring it for weeks.

Oh, no, tomorrow's Sunday. I'll have to wait all through tomorrow and go on Monday. Sunday is always the longest day of the week.

I pull my rocking chair to the stove, where my good bean soup is warming up. It's a known fact that bean soup is better the next day. I always make enough for leftovers.

I eat my soup. I have plenty of time to shovel Senator Lish's driveway before dark, before Saturday supper with the Lannons. I decide to take a nap.

From the deepest, darkest corner of my bureau I take out my deepest, darkest secret: my remaining strand of Tahitian black pearls. My pearls help me dream about Frank Moore, although his face is nothing but a blur now.

The stars are shining on a hot Mississippi night. Horses are galloping by; tuffs of sod shoot up behind them. We're under a longleaf pine, hiding from the Rebs, defenseless, yet hoping to catch a few hours' sleep. The air smells of pine, gunpowder, magnolia blossoms, and tart lemonade.

Frank isn't sick, but we're both so tired.

"I don't want you to be anything you're not at this very moment."

"If you could see me now, you wouldn't think so," I tell him sadly, as I wake with a start.

Everyone is using his old carriage house for automobiles these days. The automobile goes in the car riage stall. In the horse stalls the driving coats, hats, goggles, and gloves hang on hooks where the grain, hay, and water buckets used to be. I miss the horses. Ice trucks, mail trucks, and milk wagons are the only horse-drawn vehicles left anymore.

Where did all the horses go? How could they have disappeared so quickly? I'd have to walk out to the country to see field horses now. Mr. Cleary's Cheese and Crackers were a fine matched set of Shires. Sisters, as I recall.

It's not the same without horses.

It's late afternoon and I've shoveled out Senator Lish's driveway. The sun is setting; it's much colder. As he cranks up his Model T Ford, his wife sits in the driver's seat, ready to back the automobile out and down the driveway. Her gloved hands grasp the steering wheel with grim determination.

The early twilight turns the sky purple. The snow on the endless prairie is the palest lilac. After more than fifty years in Illinois, I still marvel at the utter flatness of the land, as flat as the palm of my hand.

Women shouldn't be allowed to drive automobiles, in my opinion. They're too excitable and not mechanically minded.

The Model T coughs once, then bursts to life.

"Back her out, then turn her right! Turn her sharp right!" Senator Lish calls out.

Why is it that men always refer to machinery as "she"? Especially if the machinery is complicated, tetchy, and hard to control?

Mrs. Lish is wearing a floppy lady's driving hat of wool felt tied up with a scarf to keep the winter wind off her face. Maybe she can't see me. The Model T shoots backward fast. Too fast.

My feet in their new galoshes slip as I try to get out of the way.

An explosion of pain in my legs . . . my hip—

I'm lying in a mound of shoveled snow. Senator and Mrs. Lish are looking at me in shock as I black out.

I wake up to nurses cutting away my trousers.

The doctor says, "Mr. Cashier, can you hear me? You're in the hospital."

"NO! NO!" I struggle to get up as he holds me down.

"Mr. Cashier, you might have broken your hip, at the very least one of your legs. You have to lie still so I can examine you."

"No! No!" My legs won't move—the pain . . .

A nurse whispers, "Doctor?"

It becomes very quiet in the hospital room. They are all staring at me amidships—the doctors, the nurses, and Mr. Lish.

It's as though all my locks have been pried open and my doors and windows forced wide. I'm trapped.

All I can do is close my eyes.

15

EVERY DAY LOOKS DIFFERENT

1913

*I*T WASN'T MY LAST SKIRT AFTER ALL.

I'm Jennie Margaret Hodgers again and in a skirt once more.

The Saunemin Hospital didn't know what to do with me once I recovered. They sent me to the Illinois Soldiers' & Sailors' Home in Quincy. As I am the only female here, I have a private room.

Every time I walk, it all comes back to me. The peculiar way a long dress always has of trailing behind at every step. The way a long stride catches up the fabric between my ankles: I have to remember to take tiny, mincing steps. And the cold—how I remember the wind off the North Channel, blowing up my skirt tail! Skirts do a sorry job of keeping the even colder prairie wind off my legs.

I have to remember to sit with my knees

186

together. I have to remember not to swear. Cigars were a habit I acquired while foraging on the Indianola Road. I've had to give them up, too.

Psychoanalysts from as far away as London and Vienna have come to see me. They want to measure my skull circumference. They tell me that a man's skull is bigger than a woman's skull. They want to know: Has mine grown bigger over the decades? Has my brain been pushing at it from the inside, while thinking manly thoughts?

The Londoner's slim fingers reach out. Are there any soft spots between my skull and scalp? As on a newborn's head?

"I was a fighting infantryman! I've worked hard all my life!" I flail at them with my walking stick. "Buster!" I shout. "Don't you make me poison your dog!"

They turn and flee. "Good riddance," I whisper.

As soon as I come into the sunroom, the old men gather around, like bees to a honey tree, to talk *at* me. I'm supposed to listen to their exploits, their tales of daring, and their breathless stories of last-minute decisions that changed the face of battle. I can tell, just by looking at them, that they'd be insulted if I told them any of *my* war stories. So I don't. I've taken to just sitting here at the window and looking at the scenery: the long stretch of grass to the lake, the prairie, and the Mississippi River beyond them.

Every day looks different. I've never noticed that before. Every day is slightly more wintry, or springlike, or summery, or autumnal, or slightly less so than the day before. It's remarkable how every day is ever so slightly different.

I don't stop sitting here, my strand of Tahitian black pearls in my hands, until I see a difference in the weather. After that, I go back to my room and take a nap.

They all think I'm crazy. Why else would a woman live in men's clothes for more than fifty years? Why would she choose to live such a hard and lonely life? Why would she volunteer to march off to war and stay in that war for more than two years?

When we're all awake, it's a quiet, peaceful room. It's the nodding off that puts us back into our various wars and battles. Dreaming patients scream from their wheelchairs. The nurses come running to wake them up.

In fair weather, ladies and schoolchildren come from the town and read newspapers to us. A schoolboy is reading the news from Europe, and it doesn't sound good. The schoolboy is so young! He reads in such a grave, ominous voice. I ask him, "Do you have a friendly dog? Would you like some cookies?"

He says, "No, thank you. Ma'am."

The Germans have finally gotten organized enough to merge into a nation. They're so pleased with themselves that they're determined to turn everyone else into Germans as well. Their Kaiser Wilhelm has threatened Belgium, France, Holland, and the United Kingdom.

Oh, everyone denies a war is coming, but we all

know better. That schoolboy reading us the news certainly knows better.

The schoolboy's curly auburn hair reminds me of Tom.

"Is that you, my own brother Tom?" I cry out. Tears funnel into the deep wrinkles around my eyes. I no longer have to hold my tears back. I can cry anytime I want.

I understand, Tom, I understand. Men must compete against men, but women are free to shower kindness on the world. I understand why my good fortune in America riled you so. You were eaten up with jealousy.

A nurse is walking toward me. I slacken my jaw and stare into space.

"Miss Hodgers, some visitors to see you."

Two old men stand in front of me.

"It's me—Robbie Horan."

"It's me—Charlie Ives."

I forget for a moment to act feeble-minded. "Charlie! Robbie! You two are still alive?"

They remain standing, looking at me expectantly.

The nurse says, "Miss Hodgers, a lady is supposed to invite gentlemen to sit." She smiles at Robbie and Charlie. "She can be forgetful."

"Well, sit down, then," I say. Their ancient knees creak and pop as they sit on opposite sides of me.

Charlie cackles and goes to slap me on the back. The skirt draped around my legs stops him.

Robbie sticks his hand out to shake mine. The ruffle on my blouse sleeve stops him.

"Well," Charlie says. "Who would have thought? You sure fooled me. All those Saturdays, when we were Belvidere farm boys? Remember? You could raise merry Hell with the best of them."

Robbie glares at him. "Don't swear in front of a lady."

"Oh . . . sorry. Um, Miss Hodgers."

"I remember," I say softly. I grin at Robbie. "Do you think I haven't heard swearing before? I was a fighting infantryman! Swear away, the two of you."

"Then go to Hell!" Robbie shouts. "We trusted you. We were men at arms, and we trusted you to fight alongside us!"

Charlie says, "She did fight alongside us."

"I never turned tail, Robbie," I say quietly. "Not even once."

"Remember Bryce's Crossroads at Tishomingo Creek Bridge?" Charlie asks. "Remember Guntown? We'd given everything we had and it still wasn't enough. My grandsons ask for war stories, but I've never once spoken of Guntown to my wife, my children, or my grandchildren. How could they possibly understand?

"Instead, I talk about Vicksburg. I went to Vicksburg back in, oh, . . . 1899 it was. Do you know they still don't celebrate Fourth of July down there? I can't say I blame them."

"I don't blame them, either," I reply. "I've never returned to the South. I had enough the first time."

Charlie gives me a hard stare. "Say something in

190

Irish. Whenever Albert was flustered or agitated, he'd say something in Irish."

"In Irish?"

"You know, in an Irish brogue. An accent."

"But I'm not flustered or agitated."

"Then go to Hell!" Robbie yells again, louder this time.

I turn on him, snarling like Buster. "You won't be saying that to me again, Robbie Horan. I fought at the Battle of Vicksburg, same as you. D'you remember when our own Lieutenant Colonel Humphrey leaped out of his coffin? White as a ghost, you were."

I lean back in my chair with a smile on my face. Charlie's right—when I'm flustered or agitated, my brogue does come back, but not often this thick. I sound like an enraged leprechaun.

"God Almighty," Charlie says. "It *is* Albert Cashier."

Charlie has a full beard, pure white—the sort of beard I'd have given anything to have in my Drummer Boy days.

"Charlie Ives! I've known you for fifty-two years, since before the war even. It's good to see you."

Charlie says, "You don't have to worry about your pension. We'll swear on Bibles that you were Albert Cashier, won't we, Robbie? I'll talk by telephone to the Bureau of Pensions at the War Office. President Wilson has gotten wind of your predicament, and he's written to the governor. The President of the United States wants you to keep your pension. We'll set things right, won't we, Robbie?"

Robbie lets out his breath. "Good day to you, Miss Hodgers."

Using his cane, he hoists himself up and walks slowly out of the sunroom. The back of his neck has a tense, indignant quality to it.

"He'll be back," Charlie says flatly. "He loves to talk about Vicksburg."

Charlie takes my hand. Wintry sunshine lights up the sunroom. We sit and share war stories for the rest of the afternoon.

Jennie Hodgers was a real person. The men she fought with in the 95th Illinois Infantry, Company G, were real people too, as were the officers, her parents, her brother, the Belvidere Clearys, the Lannons, and the Lishes.

Frank Moore is based on the 95th Illinois's historian Wales Wood. Mr. Wood survived the war. His *A History of the Ninety-fifth Regiment, Illinois Infantry Volunteers* is the definitive book on this regiment. Although Albert and Frank's attachment is fiction, Wales Wood and Albert Cashier were the best of friends. Albert is on almost every page of Mr. Wood's book.

After Albert Cashier was hit by State Senator Ira Lish's car, Jennie Hodgers was transferred to the Illinois Soldiers' & Sailors' Home in Quincy, Illinois, for long-term convalescence. She told the doctors and nurses there that she'd been born near Belfast, Ireland. She remembered collecting seashells on the Island Magee with her older brother. Jennie Hodgers started wearing pants in Ireland, when she worked as a shepherd.

She must have been born in the mid-1840s, but there was no record of her birth in her local parish.

Albert Cashier fought in many more battles than Vicksburg, Bryson's Crossroads at the Tishomingo

Creek Bridge, and the Siege of Fort Spanish on Dauphin Island. Albert fought in a guerrilla campaign on the Red River in Louisiana, at the siege of Montgomery in Alabama, and at the siege of Greenwood in Mississippi. Space did not allow me to write about these battles.

Albert Cashier volunteered to work as a courier many times during the war. Private Cashier was taken prisoner, briefly, during the siege of Vicksburg. She got into a fistfight with her captors and escaped.

The Confederate States of America's president, Jefferson Davis, called Vicksburg "the nail that holds the two pieces of the Confederacy together." The Union was as determined to take Vicksburg as the Confederacy was determined to keep it. It took eighteen months for the small town to fall to the Union.

CAMP DOUGLAS

Over 26,000 prisoners were sent to Camp Douglas, 12,000 in December 1864 alone. At least 8,000 died there. Others were sent to other prisoner-of-war camps, including Johnson's Island, Ohio, in Sandusky Bay; Lake Erie; and Rock Island, Illinois, in the middle of the Mississippi River. The harsh Great Lakes winters killed them by the thousands. The swell of prisoners overburdened the supply of goodwill, blankets, medicine, and food. Only 2,000 prisoners were sent home after signing the loyalty oath to the United States.

At the Illinois Soldiers' & Sailors' Home in Quincy, Illinois, both Robbie Horan and Charlie Ives testified under oath that Jennie Hodgers was indeed Albert Cashier so she could keep her pension after her true sex was known. She was the only woman on either side of the war known to have received a Civil War pension.

Jennie Hodgers died in the Watertown State Hospital for the Insane in East Moline, Illinois, on October 10, 1915. At her death she was suffering from what we now call Alzheimer's disease.

Her true sex was common knowledge before she died. Nevertheless, her body was dressed in her Grand Army of the Republic uniform. She was given a full military burial, including an American flag draped over her coffin. Her marker in Sunnyslope Cemetery in Saunemin, Illinois, is simple and says nothing of her complicated life.

It reads: *Albert Cashier, Co. G 95 Ill. Inf.*

––––––

What would it have been like to be Jennie Hodgers? To worry that the slightest gesture, the smallest slip of the tongue, the simplest glitch in her routine, might reveal her true identity? Could she have second-guessed everything she ever did, everything she ever thought? She must have lived such a lonely life.

To us, what Jennie Hodgers did seems unbelievable. How could she have fooled everyone, in both war and peacetime, for more than fifty years?

She grew up in a world without birth certificates, without immigration and naturalization papers, without passports or social security numbers or photo ID's, without fingerprinting or driver's licenses or DNA testing, without federal and state withholding taxes. There was no proof to say she was or wasn't who she said she was.

She left $418.46 in a bank account. That doesn't sound like much by today's standards, but in 1911 a brand-new Model T Ford cost $600.

The town of Saunemin tried to find a beneficiary in Ireland for the money. They wrote to the city government of Belfast and to the local parishes. Plenty of Hodgerses came forward, but none could place her as a relative to the satisfaction of the town.

In 1924 the town of Saunemin gave the money to Jennie Hodgers's local parish of Ballynure, near Belfast, Ireland.

SELECTED BIBLIOGRAPHY AND INTERNET SOURCES

The Belvidere Republican, Belvidere, Ill., 1864.

The Belvidere Standard, Belvidere, Ill., 1862–1864.

Blanton, DeAnne, and Lauren Cook. *They Fought Like Demons: Women Soldiers in the American Civil War.* Baton Rouge, La.: Louisiana State University Press, 2002.

Chicago Historical Society: www.chicagohs.org

Darwin, Charles. *The Voyage of the Beagle.* Garden City, N.Y.: The Natural History Library, Anchor Books/Doubleday & Company, reprinted 1962.

Fact Monster: www.factmonster.com

Foote, Shelby. *The Civil War, a Narrative.* Vol. 2: *Fredericksburg to Meridian.* Vol. 3: *Red River to Appomattox.* New York: Vintage Books/Random House, 1986.

Forgotten New York: www.forgottenny.com

Jordan, Robert Paul. *The Civil War*. Washington, D.C.: National Geographic Society, 1969.

Korn, Jerry. *War on the Mississippi: Grant's Vicksburg Campaign*. Alexandria, Va.: Time-Life Books, 1985.

Lannon, Mary Catherine. "Albert D. J. Cashier and the Ninety-fifth Illinois Infantry." Master's thesis, Illinois State University, 1969. Milner Library, Illinois State University, Normal, Ill.

Long, E. B., with Barbara Long. *The Civil War Day by Day: An Almanac, 1861–1865*. New York: The Da Capo Press, Inc., 1977; reprint of Garden City, N.Y.: Doubleday & Co., 1971 edition.

Rare Book and Special Collections Division, Library of Congress.

Rosten, Leo. *The Joys of Yiddish*. New York: McGraw-Hill, 1968.

The 29th Ohio Volunteer Infantry, Company H, Civil War reenactors.

Webb, James. *Born Fighting: How the Scots-Irish Shaped America*. New York: Broadway Books, 2004.

Wood, Wales. *A History of the Ninety-fifth Regiment, Illinois Infantry Volunteers*. Chicago: Tribune Company's Book and Job Printing Office, 1865.